I0748465

Of Woman by Woman

Sandra A. Wawrytko
General Editor

Vol. 66

PETER LANG
New York • Washington, D.C./Baltimore • Bern
Frankfurt • Berlin • Brussels • Vienna • Oxford

Of Woman by Woman

Two Erotic Novellas from Ming China

Translated with an Introduction by
R.W.L. Guisso & Lenny Hu

PETER LANG
New York • Washington, D.C./Baltimore • Bern
Frankfurt • Berlin • Brussels • Vienna • Oxford

Library of Congress Cataloging-in-Publication Data

Of woman by woman: two erotic novellas from Ming China /
translated with an introduction by R.W.L. Guisso, Lenny Hu.
p. cm. – (Asian thought and culture; v. 66)
Includes bibliographical references.
1. Erotic stories, Chinese—Translations into English. 2. Chinese fiction—
Ming dynasty, 1368–1644—Translations into English. 3. Prohibited books—China.
I. Guisso, R. W. L. II. Hu, Lenny. III. Xu, Changling. Ruyijun zhuan. English.
IV. Xu, Changling. Lord of perfect satisfaction. V. Furongzhuren. Chipozi zhuan.
English. VI. Furongzhuren. Memoir of a crazy old woman.
PL2658.E8O4 895.1'3460803538—dc22 2010033279
ISBN 978-1-4331-1073-3
ISSN 0893-6870

Bibliographic information published by **Die Deutsche Nationalbibliothek**.
Die Deutsche Nationalbibliothek lists this publication in the "Deutsche
Nationalbibliografie"; detailed bibliographic data is available
on the Internet at http://dnb.d-nb.de/.

Contents

Introduction

The two works introduced in this volume are perhaps the earliest pieces of erotic fiction in both Chinese and world literature.[1] *Lord of Perfect Satisfaction*, according to general consensus, was written somewhere in the middle period of the Jiajing reign of the Ming dynasty, roughly equivalent to the mid-sixteenth century.[2] It was fifty or more years earlier than the erotic novel *Xiuta yeshi* (The Unofficial History of the Embroidered Couch) and preceded *Fanny*

1 The term "erotic fiction" does not include erotic poems, such as Sappho's (6th century BC) on women's homosexual love (lesbianism) and the risqué Chinese lyrics collected in the earliest Chinese poetry classic *Shijing* (The Book of Poetry), and sexual manuals and discourse such as *The Kamasutra*, the ancient Hindu text partly focused on erotic pleasure, *La Cazzaria* (The Book of the Prick) by Antonio Vignali written in 1525 and translated recently by Ian Frederick Moulton, and *Sunu jing* (*Classic of the Plain Woman*), one of the ancient Chinese medical texts on sex. Since they are different generically, they are not within the scope of discussion in this Introduction. Some tales in Boccaccio's (1313–1375) *Decameron* are about sex or seduction, but detailed descriptions of copulation are largely absent in them, and so they cannot be regarded erotic fiction in the strict sense of this term.

2 Liu Hui argues that *Lord of Perfect Satisfaction* was published in the ninth year of the Zhengde reign, i.e., 1514, because the preface written by an anonymous literatus in the earliest Ming edition available to us bears the cyclical year "jiaxu," which, in his judgment, corresponds to 1514. See Liu Hui's article, "*Ruyijun zhuan* de kanke niandai jiqi yu *Jin Ping Mei* zhi guanxi" (*Lord of Perfect Satisfaction*: The Year of its Publication and its Relationship with *The Plum in the Golden Vase*). It is true that Huang Xun (1490-?), in his book *Dushu yide* (A Gleaning from Reading Books), which was published in 1562, mentioned that he had read the story. But that only means that the story itself had been written before 1562, not the preface, which could have been very possibly added when *Lord of Perfect Satisfaction* was brought out in print in the spring tide of publication of fiction and drama in the early years of the Wanli reign. So the year *jiaxu*, in which the preface was written, corresponds to 1574 rather than 1514. The story itself, as pointed out by the majority of scholars such Zheng Zhenduo, Zhang Peiheng, and Wang Xiaotao, was possibly a product of the mid-Jiajing reign. See Zhang Peiheng's article on *Lord of Perfect Satisfaction*, in *Zhongguo jinshu daguan* (Compendium of the Banned Books in China), ed., Zhang Peiheng et al., p. 312, and Wang Xiaotao's preface to *Lord of Perfect Satisfaction*, in *Mingdai xiaoshuo jikan disan ji* (Fiction of the Ming Dynasty, Series 3), vol. 6, p. 3.

Hill, a Western analogue, by almost two centuries. *Memoir of a Crazy Old Woman* came into being a little later, and its date of publication (or circulation in the form of a manuscript) might be anytime from the early to middle period of the Wanli reign (1572–1620); that is to say, in the last two decades of the sixteenth century.

During the sixteenth century in Europe, the era of the Renaissance, creative writing was no longer of the epic sort focused on the celebration of heroes, gods, martial feats, and adventures. It was more concerned with the human condition and with the vicissitudes of daily life such as the joys and sorrows of love and marriage.[3] At approximately the same time in China, a literary change, in scale and scope no less than that of the Renaissance, was also taking place,[4] and one of its more interesting facets was the emergence of a kind of fiction innovative in style and characterized by its defiance of prevailing ideological conventions and moralities. This type of fiction, with its political or religious orientation and its interest in describing generalized sensuality or even graphic scenes of bedroom enjoyment, is very different from the historical romance popular since the Yuan dynasty (1279–1368).[5] *Lord of Perfect Satisfaction* and *Memoirs of a Crazy Old Woman*, both of which were many times banned in the Qing dynasty (1644–1911) and are now still censored in China because of their "obscene" descriptions of sex, are two pioneering works representing this nascent trend in literature.

1

Lord of Perfect Satisfaction (*Ruyi jun zhuan*), is the story of Wu Zetian (624–705), a ruler sometimes compared to Catherine the Great,[6] who indulges in illicit

3 For a recent insightful discussion of Western culture, from the period of the Renaissance to the present, see Jacques Barzun, *From Dawn to Decadence: 500 Years of Western Cultural Life*, Harper-Collins (2001).

4 In the discussion of the changes in late Ming literature, the mainland scholar Ma Meixin's article "Wan Ming wenxue chutan" (A Preliminary Study of the Late Ming Literature), in *Zhongguo shoupi wenxue boshi xuewei lunwen xuanji* (Selected First Batch of PhD Dissertations on Literature), is worth reading.

5 The historical romance refers to the novel that centers around real historical figures and uses historical events as background or plot. The most well-known examples of this genre are *Sanguozhi yanyi* (Romance of the Three Kingdoms) and *Shuihu zhuan* (Water Margin). For a general discussion of the historical romance, see Lu Xun, *Zhongguo xiaoshuo shilue* (A Brief History of Chinese Fiction), chapters 14 & 15, in *Lu Xun quanji* (Complete Works of Lu Xun), pp. 127–153; for an in-depth interpretation of *Romance of the Three Kingdoms* and *Water Margin*, see C.T. Hsia, *The Classic Chinese Novel*, chapters 2 & 3.

6 Catherine II the Great (1729–1796) was notorious for her libertinism—her illicit sexual

sex with her lover Xue Aocao–the "lord of perfect satisfaction." Its real protagonist, in spite of what the title suggests,[7] is Empress Wu rather than her lover. For this reason, the story begins with an introduction to her background, and emphasizes at the very outset her seduction of the emperor Gaozong, her future husband, even though she is a concubine of his father at the time.

Though she later acknowledges a sexual compatability with her husband, it is not until she becomes a widow in 685 that she realizes that she is unwilling to spend the rest of her days in a celibate state.

In 685, she was over sixty years of age and was at the apogee of her power. She had just disinherited her son, Zhongzong, who had enjoyed the throne only for a few months, installing her youngest son as her puppet. When the story opens, she has proclaimed herself "emperor"–the only female in China's long history to take this bold step, though this event did not in fact occur until 690. The novella describes her at this time as a vigorous woman who has maintained her health so well that her body is "ripe with the voluptuous allure of a young woman," and we are told that one day, the eunuch Niu Jinqing introduces to her a young man named Xue Aocao,[8] who is endowed with a penis of extraordinary size. The Empress introduces him into the palace to provide her with sexual services, and he offers her so much pleasure that she awards him the title "Lord of Perfect Satisfaction." In time, Aocao becomes

---

relationship with numerous male favorites.

7 In fact, *Lord of Perfect Satisfaction* is only a partial title, and the original full and unabridged title is "Zetian huanghou ruyijun zhuan" (Empress Wu Zetian's Lord of Perfect Satisfaction).

8 The historical model for Xue Aocao is a virile, illiterate man called Xue Huaiyi, who, according to the *Official History of the Tang*, was unusually tall and robust, and made his living as a purveyor of herbs, cosmetics and probably sexual services to elite women in the secondary Tang capital of Luoyang. He was recommended to the empress as a man "of unusual talent," and she introduced him into the palace in spite of demands that he first be castrated, since only eunuchs and celibate clerics were permitted in the inner quarters. Her refusal to have him castrated–she had him ordained as a monk instead–gave rise immediately to rumours of a sexual liaison between them. Official sources are never explicit about the relationship, but there is no doubt that it was believed both by contemporaries and later commentators. Huaiyi served the Empress in several official capacities, most notably in the forgery of a prophetic Buddhist sutra which aided her in securing legitimation as emperor, and as the architect of her magnificent Hall of Light (*Ming-tang*). In 692, jealous of the empress' new lover (her personal physician), he burned the Hall of Light, and was subsequently murdered by a group of palace-women reputedly led by the empress' daughter, Princess Taiping. See Guisso, R.W.L., *Wu Tse-t'ien and the Politics of Legitimation in T'ang China*, Western Washington U. P. (1978), pp.35–36, *et. passim*.

not simply a purveyor of sexual gratification, but also an indispensible support to the empress. The real Aocao, according to the *Official History of the Tang Dynasty*, served her as an architect, general, and abbot of the prestigious White Horse Monastery. In the story, he takes advantage of her profound affection to urge upon her the restoration of the Tang house which she had deposed, and succeeds in persuading her to restore its true heir, her son Zhongzong, to the throne. This noble deed leads him in the end, to the attainment of Daoist immortality. The real Aocao was in fact, dead long before there was any talk of a restoration.

The novella, therefore, is based only loosely on actual history, but it does follow the general outline of actual events which occurred at the end of the seventh-century. The story is presented in a real or semi-realistic framework, and the cast of characters—the emperors, empresses, concubines, princes, courtiers, and *mianshou* (male sex-workers or gigolos, as we might call them today), are drawn largely from official or unofficial histories, and their real names appear in the novella. It goes without saying that Empress Wu and her husband Gaozong, are authentic figures, and even minor characters like the Zhang brothers, Chu Suiliang, and Di Renjie appear prominently in China's official dynastic histories.[9] Major events or incidents related to the Empress, such as her enthronement as "Emperor" after deposing two of her own sons, and even her eccentric command for flowers to bloom in winter, are well-documented. Authenticity is further preserved in the profusion of details and episodes drawn from a variety of Tang and Song sources, which give an air of verisimilitude to a story set almost a millennium before the author's own time. Rationalistic readers in the Ming period would have found it hard to give credence to the Empress' edict, composed in poetic form, that all the flowers in the palace gardens bloom in winter for her pleasure, but this edict appears on record not only in the official dynastic history, but also in a number of other works published in Tang-Song times.[10]

At the same time, however, *Lord of Perfect Satisfaction* transcends the established genre of historical romance in China.[11] It is not really the historical novel it purports to be, any more than Shakespeare's *Romeo and Juliet*

---

9 Of course, not all the details about the Zhang brothers, Chu Suiliang, and other minor historical figures in the story are authentic, and the obvious distortions of historical facts by the author of the story have been pointed out in the notes.

10 *Tangshi jishi* (Events behind the Compilation of Tang Poetry) and *Guang zhuoyi ji* (Expanded Records of the Things Strange and Extraordinary) are two examples.

11 According to Robert Hegel, "most [Chinese historical fiction] is set in periods of strife and generally narrates the rise and fall of dynasties." Robert Hegel, *Reading Historical Fiction*, Stanford U.P. (1998), p. 30.

is a genuinely historical play. War and peace, heroic exploits, and palace coups are featured in most Chinese fiction of this kind, but in *Lord of Perfect Satisfaction* they serve only as a backdrop or a narrative outline. The central concern of the short novella is a type of private history that is by and large confined to the so-called "inner court," the women's quarters of the imperial palace; and quite frequently, even to the Empress' bedchamber. The author, who, penning a narrative whose explicit eroticism has never before been seen, is in fact skillfully following the conventions of earlier Chinese historical romances in the opening sections of his tale.[12] As the story unfolds, however, he deviates ingeniously from this pattern, taking the reader from the familiar arena of political intrigues into an internal, sensual, and somewhat mystical world, which, without a consistent historical setting and concealed from the outside, delves into the realms of lust and the psyche of female sexuality, and is spiced with explicit depictions of copulation and revelry in the delights of the flesh.

Lord of Perfect Satisfaction therefore has a very special claim on the attention of modern readers: it is the first piece of Chinese fiction which presents carnality in all its fullness.

There are earlier examples of fiction where love and erotic pleasure feature prominently, though coyly; but there is no doubt that *Lord of Perfect Satisfaction* is the very first to challenge the existing taboos against explicit or graphic descriptions of sex in Chinese *belle lettres.* Such earlier stories as "Feiyan waizhuan" (The Unofficial Chronicle of Zhao Feiyan) written presumably by a certain Lingxuan of the Han dynasty,[13] or "You xianku" (Visiting the Fairies' Grotto) by Zhang Zhuo of the Tang dynasty [14] are well-known earlier works,

---

12 Formulae are the conventions which the author of the historical romance relied upon, such as the use of historical background and the creation of real and fictionalized historical figures. In *Lord of Perfect Satisfaction,* however, when the main story about the sexual relations of Empress Wu and Xue Aocao unfolds, the historical background fades away or is deliberately distorted (see the notes to the story), and the real historical figures are completely or partially replaced by fictitious personae.

13 Lu Xun doubted that "Feiyan waizhuan" was written in the Han dynasty. See Lu Xun, *Zhongguo xiaoshuo shilue,* chapter 11, p. 104. It was very likely that the work was written by an author of the Five Dynasties period (907–960).

14 This story has recently been re-translated by Paul Rouzer under the title "A Dalliance in the Immortals' Den" Harvard Asia Center (2001). The following passage is the most graphic in the story: "The night was growing late and our feelings grew more passionate and intimate. The fish-oil lamp shone bright all around; the wax candles illumined all sides. Shiniang then called for Cassia Heart and also for Peony. They took off my slippers, folded up my robe, put aside my turban, and hung up my sash. I then helped Shiniang take off her damask cape, undo her gauze skirt, shed her red chemise, remove her green stockings. Her

and though they touch upon amorous encounters, neither of them can be considered as true erotica. The encounters they describe are brief and lacking in detail, and the sexual acts they portray are veiled, and shielded by the abundant use of metaphors, symbols and euphemisms.[15] The *Lord of Perfect Satisfaction*, with its unashamed revelation of private body parts, postures of intercourse, and bawdy conversations between Empress Wu and her lover, is therefore to be considered the very first example in China, and perhaps in the wider literary world, of erotic or prurient literature. Whether or not it is pornography awaits the judgment of a time when there is consensus on the definition of that elusive term.[16]

---

flower-like features filled my eyes, and a fragrant breeze assaulted my nostrils. My heart leapt uncontrollably; passion came irrepressibly. I slid my hand into her crimson trousers while we entwined our limbs under the turquoise coverlet. We held our mouths lip to lip, while I supported her head with my arm. I fondled and squeezed her breasts, rubbed and stroked her thighs. A nip brought elated feelings, an embrace brought a broken heart. My nostril throbbed, and my heart was tied in knots. Before long my eyes were blurred and my ears burned, my veins bulged and sinews grew slack." See Paul Rouser, *Articulated Ladies: Gender and the Male Community in Early Chinese Texts*, Harvard U.P. (2001), pp. 348–349.

15 Whether or not the love stories in the corpus of Tang romance have a direct bearing on the appearance of *Lord of Perfect Satisfaction* is an issue worthy of further exploration. But it seems more fruitful if we expand our study of this first piece of erotic work to consider the factors outside the scope of generic intertextuality, such as the sexual over-indulgence of Emperor Wuzhong (r. 1506–1521), the politics in the early period of Jiajing reign (1522–1566), the strong interest in the art of the bedchamber along with the widespread use of aphrodisiacs, and the looser restriction on people's freedom of speech due to Emperor Shizong's (r. 1522–1566) noninterference (*wuwei er zhi*) policies and the devotion of most of his time to Daoist pursuits. These aspects of the late Ming, are well-described in Mote, F. W., *Imperial China*, Harvard U.P. (1999), pp.723 ff. See also Wile, D., *The Art of the Bedchamber*, S.U.N.Y. Press, (1992), for a thoroughgoing discussion of sexual handbooks in the late Ming, and Emperor Shizong's interest in them.

16 In both medical and erotic writing in China, authors avoided explicit vocabulary in referring to the sexual act or to body parts in a sexual context, instead using such terminology as "clouds and rain" (coitus), "jade object or jade stalk" (penis), "jasper or jade gate" (vagina) etc. In the two translations here, *Lord* tends to use more colorful euphemisms than does *Memoir* where the language is more "matter-of-fact". Hence, the authoress of the latter generally refers to female and male body parts in terms of *yin* and *yang*. Our glossary presents a comparison of the sexual terms used in both stories.

Euphemistic expression, a common feature of such better-known works as *The Plum in the Golden Vase* and *The Carnal Prayer Mat*, is one reason why these works, like *Lord* and *Memoir*, are considered erotica rather than pornography. *The Embroidered Couch*, on the other hand, uses such blunt and vulgar terms as "*luan*" (cock) and "*bi*" (cunt), not just in sexual scenes, but in the everyday conversation of the characters. This work has always been considered pornography rather than erotica. Modern considerations, such as whether or not a work's sole purpose is that of sexual titillation or whether it has 'redeeming social

Sexual fiction seems nowadays to have become a field too well-plowed. Four hundred years ago, however, the field was still virgin soil. Xu Changling, the pseudonymous author of *Lord of Perfect Satisfaction,* might therefore be considered a pioneer in the truest sense of that overworked word. His, however, is not a name found in standard histories of Chinese literature, and his real identity, despite a belated curiosity in recent decades about him and his notorious story,[17] has remained unknown except for a few generally-accepted facts. He was a native of the Ming prefecture of Suzhou[18] and flourished during the mid-sixteenth century[19] He is referred to in the preface of the *Jin Ping Mei* (The Plum in the Golden Vase), as a literatus of "a previous generation." Beyond these bare facts, we know nothing, and can only lament the fact that as the founder of this sub-genre of Chinese literature, he languishes in obscurity.

For this reason, few scholars of literature are aware that the tradition of lustful, full-flavored fiction in the late Ming period began with this slender piece of work by a largely unknown pseudonymous author. Classical though its language may be, at that time it was revolutionary in terms of its explicit sexuality, and it came to be admired by erotic novelists of later periods, including the authors of *The Plum in the Golden Vase, The Embroidered Couch,* and *The Carnal Prayer Mat.* Viewing it as the *locus classicus* for those who wished to write erotic tales, later authors often quoted in their works certain words, phrases, or sentences, and even copied its more lurid passages verbatim. Some even listed it as one of the required readings for newly-wed

---

value," as a line of demarcation between erotica and pornography are explored at several points in this Introduction. For a fairly comprehensive list of euphemisms in Chinese texts, see *The Tao of Sex: A Chinese Introduction to the Arts of the Bedchamber,* Ishhihara, A. and H. S. Levy, Shibundo, (1968), pp. 161–63.

17 A number of articles in Chinese appeared in the last twenty years or so, on the subject of *Lord of Perfect Satisfaction,* and are listed in the Selected Bibliography. We were also aware that Charles Stone had been working on *Ruyijun zhuan* for some time, but our translation had been completed before Stone published his revised PhD thesis under the title *The Fountainhead of Chinese Erotica: Lord of Perfect Satisfaction* in 2003. His study, with a different approach, is worth reading, though it is perhaps a little too academic for the general reader.

18 On the title page of the novella the author's name, Xu Changling, is preceded by two characters *Wumen,* which indicate that he was a native of the prefecture of Suzhou.

19 The preface to *Jin Ping Mei* (The Plum in the Golden Vase) indicates clearly that *Lord of Perfect Satisfaction* appeared after *Bingzhu qingdu* (Plain Talking by the Candle) by Zhou Jingxuan, who, according to Zhang Peiheng, belonged mainly to the Jiajing reign. It is thus very likely that the author of *Lord of Perfect Satisfaction* also flourished during the Jiajing reign. See Zhang Peiheng et al., *op.cit.,* p. 312.

women,[20] and most acknowledged directly or indirectly that they wrote under its influence and were, to a certain extent, the heirs to its erotic heritage.

Two characteristics of erotic fiction, first appearing in *Lord of Perfect Satisfaction*, became almost standard in later examples of the *genre*.

The first is the alleged female fascination with penis size. Previous literature, including the long Chinese tradition of manuals of sexual practice and hygiene, invariably approached sexual pleasure and its benefits solely from a male perspective. This is most clearly seen in Douglas Wile's *Art of the Bedchamber*.[21] What we see in *Lord of Perfect Satisfaction* is an entirely different picture: a woman admiring and enjoying a man with a "huge endowment." Unlike the female protagonists in earlier works, Empress Wu Zetian loves Aocao not simply because he is handsome and romantic, but because he possesses an organ "the prodigious size of which verged on abnormality." It is so huge, and provides the Empress with such great delight, that it makes her realize what she truly wants from a man.

If the well-known expositors of sexual psychology, Eberhard and Phyllis Kronhausen, are correct in suggesting that one of the typical features of sexual fiction is its strong interest in the function of an unusually large penis in intimidating or conquering a female,[22] then we might here modify their thesis by adding one more dimension. This story, the "fountainhead" of inspiration for the depiction of large penile erections in Chinese erotica, is actually more about the role of the phallus in arousing female passion, than it is about the portrayal of genital size for the sake of flaunting virile strength and dominating a female partner.

The second characteristic which later became something of a convention, is the fantasy of aberrant and excessive sexual behaviors. Xu Changling actually celebrates or valorizes a form of desire which goes beyond "normal" limits, and presents in his picture of Wu Zetian an insatiable sensualist, almost a nymphomaniac, rather than what the reader may have expected—a majestic but elderly woman with an understandable but restrained erogenous impulse. Toward the end of the story, the empress is over seventy, but she is portrayed as so robust and lustful, and so filled with sexual energy, that even men much younger than herself cannot satisfy her in bed.[23] The two Zhang Brothers, for

20 See respectively chapters 18, 19, 27, 29, 37, 50, 51, 52, 61, 73, 78, and 79 of *The Plum in the Golden Vase*, Part II of *The Embroidered Couch*, and chapter 3 of *The Carnal Prayer Mat*.

21 Wile, D. *op. cit.*

22 Kronhausen, E. and P., *Pornography and the Law: the Psychology of Erotic Realism and Pornography*, Ballantine (1959), p. 221.

23 It is not altogether uncommon for an elderly woman to have strong sexual desires and a competence which grows from experience. Empress Wu has long been viewed as an

instance, are about fifty years younger than she, outstanding for the size of their male organs and stamina, but neither of them, even taking turns to "serve" her on a nightly basis, can "maintain their erection" in intercourse with her. Aocao is the sole exception; and with him the empress can indulge herself "for hours on end," though even an encounter of this length is not enough. It is only when she is able to fulfill her sensual and exhibitionist whims by straddling Aocao and engaging in intercourse in that position while strolling in the palace garden with a band of musicians all around them; or, on another occasion, when she somewhat sadistically burns her lover's penis to force him to acknowledge his great love for her, does she feel both fully gratified and sexually replete.

Whether or not the author himself was similarly "perverse," or to put it more kindly, similarly " adventurous," no one knows for sure, and it seems of little importance. No one would deny, however, the fact that *Lord of Perfect Satisfaction*, with its proclivity for what is generally considered perversion, was much ahead of its time in portraying aberrant sexual conduct, and served as the inspiration in later bawdy stories and novels, for an entire panoply of uncommon and "queer" sexual activities such as incest, anal intercourse, same-sex behaviors, "swinging," wife-swapping, orgies, and an almost infinite variety of sub-categories of "normal" sexuality.

The boundary between the "normal" and "abnormal" in the realm of sexuality is, of course, a frangible one.

Until the path-breaking publication of Robert van Gulik's *Sexual Life in Ancient China* in 1961,[24] the perception in the West was that Chinese sexuality was an intensely private matter—entirely conventional in its practices, and restricted solely to procreation. In China, rigorous censorship by the Qing dynasty and throughout the Republican and Communist periods had

---

"abnormal" old bawd, but history tells us she is only one of numerous well-known females to engage in romantic and/or sexual liaisons with younger lovers. More recently, an American sexagenarian profiled in the *Vancouver Sun*, began advertising for younger sexual partners in the *New York Review of Books*. She related in the interview how she engaged in phone sex, salacious e-mails, and "dates" with men much younger than her 66 years. She claimed that she wanted to "have a lot of sex" before she turned 67 the next year. The most youthful of her lovers was a 32-year-old man whom she dated along with three other men. See Marcus Warren, "Sex with a Sexagenarian," *The Vancouver Sun*, May 12, 2003, p. c1-c3.

24 Van Gulik, R.H., *Sexual Life in Ancient China: A Preliminary Survey of Chinese Sex and Society from ca. 1500 B.C. till 1644 A. D., with a New Introduction and Bibliography by Paul. R. Goldin*, Brill (2005). Van Gulik pointed out the total lack of such studies both in Chinese and Western languages, and though he acknowledged the need, regarded his work as so potentially controversial that he printed only fifty copies for museums and academic institutions.

contributed to a similar view among the Chinese. Even today, sex education in Chinese schools is the exception rather than the norm, and many works of mildly-erotic fiction are banned as "spiritual pollution."[25]

Van Gulik's works changed the standard view, and subsequent scholarship has amplified, refined, and sometimes challenged his perceptions. Joseph Needham, for instance, rejected van Gulik's views on Daoist sexual practices and what he called "sexual vampirism" in intercourse.[26] Nonetheless, van Gulik's principal conclusion remains valid, and is worth repeating in his own eloquent words:

> ...the fundamental concept determining the ancient Chinese attitude to sex, [was] an unreserved, joyful acceptance of all the varied aspects of human procreation, ranging from the smallest biological details of carnal congress to the most elevated spiritual love of which that congress is the seal and confirmation. Viewed as the human counterpart of the cosmic creative process, sexual intercourse ...hallowed the flesh, never considered an abomination. No difference was felt, for instance, between the rain sprinkling the fields and the semen fecundating the womb; or between the rich, wet soil ready for the seed, and the moist vagina of the woman prepared for sexual congress...[27]

This speaks, of course, to the notion that among the Chinese, the sexual act itself was natural, and not an occasion of sin, shame or guilt even if it was performed for purposes other than procreation.

What then, was "abnormal" sex in Ming China?

In his extensive study of three-hundred Ming erotic prints, van Gulik provides visual evidence that positions of intercourse were varied, though fully 80% would be considered "normal," if sometimes a little inventive, by today's standards.[28] The remaining 20% depict anal and oral sex; and of this proportion, only 2% show what van Gulik calls "freak positions"—group sex, sex in a swing, and lesbianism. He finds no examples of male-male sex.

---

25 On the most recent list, and restricting ourselves only to works available in translation, are such works as *La la la* by Mianmian, *Shanghai Baby: A Novel* by Wei Hui, *Beijing Doll* by Chunshu, *Wild Ginger: A Novel*, by Anchee Min, *Whispers and Moans:Interviews with the Men and Women of Hong Kong's Sex Industry* by Yeeshan Yang, among others. Pseudonyms are used almost universally. Movies, television shows and internet blogs and fiction with sexual content are routinely banned. The most recent victim is *Snail House (Moju)*, China's most popular soap opera, removed from the airwaves in January, 2010. The official explanation was that it was too "sexy," though the real reason lay probably in its unfavorable depiction of government corruption and government failure to contain spiraling real estate costs.

26 Needham, J., *Science and Civilization in China, Vol. 11*, Cambridge U.P., 1954- (7 volumes), Vol. II, P. 146.

27 Van Gulik, *op.cit.* p. 333.

28 Van Gulik, *op.cit.* p. 330.

To the extent that these proportions represent actual practice, both the novellas appearing here contain far more than their share of activities beyond the norm!

We might finally, distinguish between "abnormal" and "illicit" sexual acts. In Ming China, adultery was a criminal act, though strictly speaking, it was a crime which only a married woman could commit. Married men could consort freely with prostitutes, and with their concubines, and only if they had sex with a married woman were they culpable. Wu Zetian, as a widow, saw her relationship with her various *mianshou* or gigolos as perfectly licit, though as a challenge to the existing double standard, it no doubt scandalized the people both of her own time and of the Ming. In both dynasties, the most shocking, and the most heavily-punished of illicit sexual behaviors, was incest. Every one of the traditional Chinese law codes spells out harsh and explicit sanctions based on the degree of familial relationship of the participants. Zetian's seduction of Gaozong was illicit even though she is not the principal wife, but only a concubine of his father at the time. Enuo, the protagonist of *Memoir*, not only commits adultery, but has relations with both her father-in-law and her three brothers-in-law.

Even more than the graphic sexuality, then, it is probably the depiction of incest which accounts for the notoriety, past and present, of both works.

Incest is not a major theme of *Lord of Perfect Satisfaction*. Its central theme and chief artistic goal is the representation of the wide spectrum of lust. It became notorious, therefore, for its bold subversion of genteel literature. But that is not all. The unconventionality of the story goes much beyond its eroticism. If one turns from its intriguing potpourri of coitus to contemplate the serious yet implicit message it intends to convey, one finds a clear sub-theme. Among other things, the work may be read as a comment on Wu Zetian as a "feminist,"[29] or at least as a proto-feminist, in her frank and demanding posture toward female sexual desire!

---

29 The terms "feminist" or "female" or "feminine" are here used as defined by Toril Moi. "What is the meaning of the word 'feminist' in feminist literary criticism? Over the past decade, feminists have used the terms 'feminist', 'female' and 'feminine' in a multitude of different ways. One of the main points of this essay, however, is to urge that only a clear understanding of the differences between them can show what the crucial political and theoretical issues of contemporary feminist criticism really are. Initially, I will suggest that we distinguish between 'feminism' as a political position, 'femaleness' as a matter of biology and 'femininity' as a set of culturally defined characteristics." See Toril Moi, "Feminist, Female, Feminine", in *The Feminist Reader*, eds., Catherine Belsey & Jane Moore, Basil Blackwell, (1989), p. 117.

Zetian, as some historians argue, was a seventh-century prototype of later strong women who struggled to bring about a greater degree of equality, freedom and equal rights for themselves.[30] Certainly it is true that prior to her audacious seizure of the throne in her own name, she ruled first as an equal, then as the dominant partner with her husband, the emperor Gaozong. Unlike the politically-involved imperial women who preceded her, she refused to rule "from behind the screen," but displayed her talents with panache and in a very public (and scandalous) way. Her long career saw numerous measures we might consider as "feminist" or at least sympathetic to the cause of woman. She challenged existing *mores*, for example, by extending the prescribed mourning period for mothers so that it became equal to the previously-longer period for fathers. She forbade the sale of unwanted daughters, and participated like a man in major state ceremonials including the grandest of all—the *feng* and *shan* sacrificial rites performed at the foot and on the summit of Mount Tai.[31] Finally, defying all tradition, she proclaimed herself "Holy Mother Emperor Divine" in 690 A.D., changing the dynastic name from Tang to Zhou. She thus became the one and only female emperor in China's long history. And needless to say, later historians and scholars, all of them male, branded her as a ruthless usurper, and as an outlaw both in her politics and in her sexuality.

The author of *Lord of Perfect Satisfaction* seems to have accepted this orthodox stereotype of a "bad" woman who exceeded the proper role assigned to her sex,[32] and in portraying her regime, emphasizes her pitiless personal vendettas, her bloody suppression of her opponents, and her deliberate exploitation of bureaucratic factionalism to enhance her own power.[33] The story therefore mocks her by quoting a verse that caricatures her as a hen (rather than a rooster) "crowing in the vacated Purple Mansion," and fiercely attacks her for the employment of cruel minions like Lai Junchen and SuoYuanli in slaughtering members of the Tang royal house and other political dissidents.

---

30 See Guisso, R.W.L., *op.cit.*, and Lei Jiaji, *Humei pianneng huozhu* (Her Fox-like Allure Captivated her Master), as well as his *Wu Zetian zhuan* (Biography of Wu Zetian).

31 On this occasion and others, Empress Wu is said to have dressed herself as a male emperor. See Lei Jiaji, *Humei pianneng huozhu*, p. 161.

32 The harshest critic of Wu Zetian was Lin Yutang (1895–1976), whose historical novel *Lady Wu—A True Story*, published in London in 1957, goes so far as to suggest that Empress Wu was a mass murderer comparable to Stalin or Chinggis Khan. The claim, of course, is ridiculous, but is indicative of the hostility toward her often felt by traditional and orthodox scholars.

33 See *Cambridge History of China: Volume 3, Sui and Tang China*, 589–906, Part I, Denis Twitchett, ed., "Kao Tsung and the Empress Wu: the Inheritor and the Usurper," p. 243.

However, despite its criticism of the Empress as a female ruler, *Lord of Perfect Satisfaction* shows an undisguised sympathy when it comes to the depiction of her sexual life. The historical record validates the view that even at an advanced age, she had not lost her interest in sex, and it was generally believed that the so-called "Institute of the Crane" which she established in her later years, and staffed with young men like the Zhang brothers, was little more than a male harem. Our author even remarks with some hyperbole, that "no one, whether the veteran prostitute or the lascivious wench, was able to equal her in lewdness." But like other fictional late -Ming *femmes fatales* who loved sensual amusements and disdained moral restraints, the Empress in our story regarded her passions not as "lewdness" or "wantonness," but rather as integral to her valid rights. "Even birds of the air know how to enjoy their conjugal relations," she sighs. "How can we humans be deprived of such pleasures?"[34]

And in enjoying her pleasures, she is no shrinking violet. No sooner, for instance, has Aocao disrobed for the first time in her presence, than she reaches out with both hands to fondle him. "How huge this beastly thing is!" she exclaims, while swiftly unbuttoning her own robes to reveal herself to him. Without hesitation, she urges him, who has not yet dared to touch her, to stroke her "conduit of pleasure." What is more, she seems to look upon her engagement of young male partners as a sort of payback in a quest to achieve equality with the man who had previously used her for his own satisfaction and had failed to consider her own needs. "I still recollect," she tells Aocao as they make love, "that when I was twenty-six or twenty-seven years old, I began to serve [my husband] Gaozong. He was much larger and more virile [than yourself] so far as that part of him is concerned. But every time he had sex with me, he cared only for his own enjoyment. Scarcely ever was he so considerate as to start or stop out of any concern for my own gratification."

It is of little wonder, therefore, that after having ascended the throne, the Empress assumes not only the political power of a male sovereign, but also asserts in the boudoir, prerogatives usually reserved to the male. She selects men of her liking, and regardless of their own wishes, compels them to please her, rather than vice versa.[35]

34 These two sentences, with little change, were used by the late-Ming playwright Tang Xianzu (1550–1616) in his famous play *Mudan ting* (The Peony Pavilion). Tang's play, widely acclaimed for its understanding of the female condition and the desire of most women for conventional love and a happy marriage, represents the new trend toward humanistic literature in the late Ming, which, to a considerable degree, resulted from the influence of *Lord of Perfect Satisfaction*.

35 As early as in the sixteenth century, the scholar Huang Xun noted Wu Zetian's "feminist"

Zetian, however, is not the stereotypical castrating female whose "feminist" sexual crusade is inspired by a crude Freudian sort of "penis envy." Though she rejects long-standing Chinese traditions of female subordination outside the confines of the home, she is by no means a woman who hates men. Her search for sexual gratification may seem on the surface, to be selfish and hedonistic, but at the same time, and with the right man, she is a passionate and unselfish lover. When the novella glides from graphic voluptuousness to lyrical sentimentality, we are shown a completely different Wu Zetian; a Wu Zetian who treats the Zhang Brothers generously in spite of their inability to measure up to her standards in the bedroom, and a Wu Zetian who dotes on Xue Aocao as though she were a maiden experiencing the first bloom of love. First, she weeps over the small burn she has inflicted on his genitals, and then, remorseful and heartbroken, writes to him a tear-stained love-letter proclaiming her sincere and profound affection. In short, we see in these incidents a side of her not readily apparent elsewhere; a facet of her personality which is caring, tender, and docile—the very attributes commonly associated with what we call "femininity."

This rather sympathetic posture of the author toward his heroine's demand for sexual freedom and control over her own body, is shown most clearly in the unexpected denouement of the story. Prior to this in Chinese literature, as in cautionary tales the world over, indulgence in sexually deviant behavior often results in some form of retribution. In many cases, the punishment is death, with no hope of salvation. As we have suggested, *Lord of Perfect Satisfaction* is ambivalent in its portrayal of Empress Wu, seeing her as an amalgam of Machiavellian political ruthlessness combined with a striking femininity; and of course, a woman with strong but natural biological urges. In the end, she is exonerated and suffers no punishment. Her illicit lover, Aocao, suffers not retribution but reward, and in an astonishing reversal of the existing conventions of traditional morality, becomes a holy recluse, seeking happily his own oneness with the *Dao*.

This scenario, which must have been conceived at the risk of the author's social ostracism, seems to serve for him as an ideological climax. Though

---

tendencies in her private life. Wu Zetian, he remarks, was very different from the other two most notorious imperial women of the Tang period since they did not balk even at incest to please powerful men. Only Wu Zetian, he points out, dared to take the initiative and play an active role in setting up her sexual liaisons. See *Dushu yide* (A Gleaning from reading Books), *juan* 2. A well-researched novel (Conney, E. and Altieri, D., *Deception: A novel of Murder and Mystery in Ancient China*, Avon, 1993), relates her proactive approach to sexual gratification in fictional form.

superficially a conservative "royalist" like Balzac,[36] he seems to have prided himself upon his understanding of the female condition of his heroine, and did not see that as incompatible with his insistence on her abdication and the restoration of the Tang dynasty. Implicitly, he acknowledges the illegitimacy of her regime, and by so-doing, perhaps diffuses the criticism which would have been leveled against him by his peers for the graphic sexuality of his work. A balance was thus achieved. His narrative strategy was one which satisfied conventional political morality, yet left him free to reject both the existing sexual code and the literary code which veiled all depiction of sexual activity. Sexual gratification, however graphic and unrestrained, did not call out for punishment.

Chinese scholars with textual training have ignored these aspects of the work, and have been inclined to interpret the story on the level of political allegory. On another level, however, it is a work whose central theme is female sexuality, and thus represents a radical departure from traditional literary prudery. It is an implicit and unprecedented *apologia* for Zetian's sexual openness, and thus can be read symbolically as a plea for the sexual liberation of women in the late-Ming as well. In fact, it was probably on this second level, that the novella made such a huge impact on contemporary Ming literati.

Among these literati, we believe, there existed a certain female author, known only by her pen-name of Madam Hibiscus. Sometime shortly thereafter, she would make her own contribution to the tradition established by *Lord*, and pen her own equally-lurid memoir. It is no coincidence that she included prominently in them, two lines composed by the Empress Wu and cited in *Lord of Perfect Satisfaction*!

2

Memoir of a Crazy Old Woman, (*Chipozi zhuan*), is perhaps the earliest erotic work penned by a female author in world literature. In some respects, it reminds us of what is usually considered the earliest novel in literary history, Lady Murasaki Shikibu's *Tale of Genji*, (*Genji Monogatari*), which first appeared around 1008.[37] In comparison to *Genji*, a true classic and the most widely-read

---

36 Honore Balzac (1799–1850), whose most famous novels are *Eugénie Grandet*, *Le Pere Goriot*, and *La Cousine Bette*, portrays, in his fiction, the rise and triumph of the third estate (the bourgeoisie) with much sympathy, though politically he was a royalist.

37 The *Tale of Genji* contains a number of sexual situations. However, in most cases, the eroticism of these scenes is implicit, and presented in metaphoric poetic form. The following flirtation between Genji and an elderly lady called Naishi is a good example.

They talked for a time. Genji was nervous lest they be seen, but Naishi was

volume in Japan from the Heian period to the present, *Memoir of a Crazy Old Woman* has won little renown. In fact, judging from the paucity of later references to it, it remained virtually unknown. While the *Genji* was read aloud to the Japanese Emperor and his courtiers throughout the twelfth-century, *Memoir* seem to have had only the most limited circulation. Since there were few female writers of any sort in Ming China, and none that we know of who were authors of fiction, literary historians have not only neglected the novella, but have never raised the question of its female authorship.[38] This failure is due in the first place to the insufficient attention paid to "Madam Hibiscus"[39] as a pseudonym. Literary historians have simply assumed male authorship, and disregarded the feminine *nom de plume*, since in their eyes, female authorship of such a work was simply unimaginable.

Works of fiction which appeared in the Late Ming, especially those nowadays categorized as erotica, were published without exception under pseudonyms.[40] The most familiar example is perhaps *The Plum in the Golden Vase*, which was attributed to an author called "The Scoffing Scholar of Lanling" (Lanling Xiaoxiao sheng), who, despite many scholars' laborious research, has remained an enigma until recent years.[41] But no matter what

---

unperturbed.

"Sere and withered though these grasses be,
They are ready for your pony, should you come."

She was really too aggressive.

"Were mine to part the low bamboo at your grove,
It would fear to be driven away by other ponies."

See *The Tale of Genji*, trans. Edward Siedensticker, p. 125.

38 During the last two decades there have been at least half a dozen articles written by Chinese scholars on *Memoir of a Crazy Old Woman*. None of them suggests female authorship.

39 The name "Madam Hibiscus" consisted originally of four Chinese characters, *furong zhuren*, meaning literally "possessor of hibiscus". Whether hibiscus refers to a beautiful face or to a flowery vagina, its "possessor" would seem certainly to be female.

40 More attempts need to be made on the part of the scholars on both sides of the Pacific to study pseudonyms in the authorship of Ming fiction.

41 A roster of names of scholars living in the Jiajing and Wanli reigns, including famous sixteenth-century literary figures such as Li Kaixian (1502-1568), Li Zhi (1527-1602), Wang Shizhen (1528-1590), Tu Long (1542-1605), Zhao Nanxing (1550-1628), and Tang Xianzu (1550-1616) has been proposed as possible authors for *The Plum in the Golden Vase* since the early 1980s. For a well-informed survey in English of the authorship studies of the novel, see Plaks, A., *The Four Master Works of the Ming Novel*, Princeton U.P. (1987), pp. 55-72.

Hu Lingyi (Lenny Hu) has in recent years, published a series of articles in Chinese suggesting that its author was Xu Wei (1521-1593) and the novel is about a real historical personage—a very high-ranking official—in the Jiajing reign. For detailed information, see

kind of masks the authors wore and no matter how difficult it is to ascertain their real identities, the pseudonyms leave little doubt as to gender. The "Scoffing Scholar of Lanling" is universally considered to be male, and so too are all other pseudonymous authors—the "Master of Perverse Love" and the "Taoist Priest for Redressing Intemperate Passion,"[42] among others. There is no single work of fiction in the Ming period, other than *Memoir of a Crazy Old Woman*,[43] which appeared under a female pseudonym!

To emphasize this point, we must be clear that the pseudonym is indeed feminine. Aside from the obvious fact that no male author of the time would identify with a flower, there was a long literary tradition in China in which the hibiscus, a species of lotus, was often used as a symbol or metaphor for a beautiful woman.[44]

And it must finally be emphasized, as both Dorothy Ko and Susan Mann have so clearly demonstrated, it was by no means unusual for educated women to write in a variety of *genres* during the late-Ming and early-Qing periods.[45]

---

the Selected Bibiography.

42 The "Master of Perverse Love" (*qingdian zhuren*) is Wang Jide (1564?-1623?), the author of *The Embroidered Couch*, and the "Daoist Priest for Redressing Intemperate Passion" (*qingchi fanzheng daoren*) is Li Yu (1611?-1681?), the author of *The Carnal Prayer Mat*. The authorship of *The Embroidered Couch* has long been attributed to Lu Tiancheng (1578?-1617?), but Lenny Hu has recently proposed that its real author was Wang Jide.

43 Masculine pseudonyms were used without exception by male authors. For example, Jikongguan zhuren (Master of the Temple of Emptiness) was Ling Mengchu (1580–1644), the author of *Two Slaps*, and Mohanzhai zhuren (Master of Ink-Crazy Studio) was Feng Menglong (1576–1646?), the author of *Three Words*. For details of Ling Mengchu's pseudonym, see the Introduction to *In the Inner Quarters: Erotic Stories from Ling Mengchu's Two Slaps*, translated by Lenny Hu and R.W.L. Guisso. The only other person also employing a feminine pseudonym was Zhiyanzhai, the commentator, not the author, of *Shitou ji* (Story of the Stone), who, Lenny Hu has proposed, was also a female. She was, he suggests, none other than the author's wife. *Story of the Stone* or *Dreams of the Red Mansion* was not a novel written in the eighteenth century as most people believe, but was largely written in the late Ming and not completed until the early Qing. The real author was Zhang Dai (1597–1684?), an erudite scholar from a very distinguished family in Shaoxing in present-day Zhejiang province.

44 According to the Chinese dictionary *Cihai* (Sea of Words), *furong* (hibiscus) is an alternative name for *lianhua* (lotus). It has been often used to describe female beauty. Nowadays *furong* refers only to the species of lotus growing on dry land, not underwater. See *Cihai*, p. 554. It seems from other examples that in Ming times, the term *furong* could be used interchangeably with *lianhua*, the term used for the underwater variety.

45 Ko, D., *Teachers of the Inner Chamber: Women and Culture in Seventeenth-century China*, Stanford U.P. (1994) and Mann, S., *Precious Records: Women in China's Long Eighteenth Century*, Stanford U.P. (1997).

Nor are there any commentators who have recognized the autobiographical nature of the novella, nor linked the feminine pseudonym to the heroine of the story.

Long ago, the anonymous author of *My Secret Life* [46] made the audacious conjecture in the preface to his pornographic diary, that he considered it likely that *Fanny Hill* was "written by a woman."[47] He offers no supporting evidence for this rather casual suggestion, but in the case of *Memoir of a Crazy Old Woman,* there is ample evidence, both internal and external, to support the assertion of female authorship.

To begin, we need to look at the word *ji* which follows the author's name on the cover of the original edition. Literally meaning "compile," *ji* seems a little misleading since it conveys to the reader that "Madam Hibiscus" was not the author, but the "compiler," of the story; and indeed, the novella is in the "as told to..." format. In the story, the "compiler" is called Yan Qiongke, and his/her very name provides us with important evidence as to authorship of the story. The structure of the narrative is such that the story's compiler interviews Chipozi (the crazy old woman), make notes on her account of her life, and "compiles" her narration into the written word, accessible to readers.

The compiler's name, Yan Qiongke, has been assumed by previous commentators to be male, but in fact, the name is gender-neutral and can be taken as either male or female.[48] It is our position that the name is female, and is a clever reference to the author herself. In our view, she is, in essence, "compiling" her own autobiography.

We base this view principally on the internal evidence of the story.

In it, as we shall see, the protagonist is a native of "Yan," a region which corresponds roughly to present-day Hebei province. Due to her advanced age, she walks with the aid of a "*qiong*," a bamboo staff or cane, and has moved away from her native place to her current home. In Chinese, migrants from one province or region to another, are called "*ke*," or guests.

It is for this reason, that we believe that the "compiler," an immigrant from Yan who walks with a cane, is a veiled reference to the protagonist

46 Ian Moulton claims that Henry Spencer Ashbee, the well-known Victorian sexologist, is the author of *My Secret Life*. See his Introduction to *La Cazzaria: The Book of the Prick*, p. 2. Moulton does not explain whether or not he has found new evidence to support his allegation.

47 See *My Secret Life*, p. 18.

48 Some might argue that in the story, the "compiler," Yan Qiongke, is referred to as *zi*, and since *zi* is commonly an honorific form of address for a male, Yan Qiongke must therefore be a man. In fact, *zi*, as an honorific form of address, can be applied to both male and female.

herself, who, as the story tells us, moved as a guest (*ke*) in her later years from Yan to a region called Zheng-Wei, which is on the border of Henan-Hebei, not too far from her native place. Moreover, at seventy, she is permanently crippled by age, and so uses a staff to walk.

The similarities are too close to be coincidence. If we assume that the interviewer, Yan Qiongke, is female, and that she is, in fact, interviewing herself, it seems to follow also that not only are Chipozi and Yan Qiongke one and the same, but that both serve simply as the alter ego of Madame Hibiscus herself![49]

Further examination of textual, as well as extra-textual evidence will help confirm this contention. According to the story, Chipozi, when she was young, was a "beauty," and even in her twilight years, still retained her "elegant manner and graceful bearing." The name she was given, "Enuo," which means "lovely" or "alluring," seems appropriate. Similarly, the name "Madam Hibiscus" suggests the beauty of the author, and as her pseudonym implies, her beauty was comparable to that of the hibiscus flower.[50]

The similarities do not end with appearances, but extend to commonalities in their educational backgrounds. Enuo, in the story, "studied the poems of the Zhou dynasty" for years, and despite her parents' injunction not to recite them aloud because of their erotic nature, "read them silently and in secret without their knowledge." Correspondingly, Madam Hibiscus seems also to have enjoyed an easy familiarity with these same poems which were gathered into the *Shijing*, or Classic of Poetry. While it is common for Chinese authors of fiction to sprinkle their prose with allusions to all five of the classics, we find in the narrative of Madame Hibiscus no fewer than twenty verses, lines, or phrases from the *Shijing* and no reference whatsoever to any of the other four classics.[51] The number of allusions is rather surprising in view of the short length of the work, and it is interesting, moreover, that most of the quotations come from the Zheng and Wei sections of the work, traditionally considered to be the most salacious, and the very sections in which Enuo showed the greatest interest.

It should be noted that educated women of the Ming, unlike educated men, seldom studied all of the classics, but usually restricted themselves to the

---

49 For elaboration of this argument, see Lenny Hu, "*Chipozi zhuan de zuozhe wenti*" (On the Authorship of *Memoir of a Crazy Old Woman*), *Ming-Qing xiaoshuo yanjiu* (Journal of Research on Ming-Qing Fiction), no. 1, 2006.

50 In the second part of the story, Father-in-law remarks as he sees Enuo emerging from her bathtub: "Ha! A lotus flower (i.e., hibiscus) emerges from a pond!" His words explicitly suggest the connection between the author's pseudonym and the heroine herself.

51 See footnotes, *passim*.

Classic of Poetry, and of course, some Ming women became noted poets. This is yet another indication of the female authorship of the work.

One can find yet another and very specific point of identity between Enuo and Madam Hibiscus in their shared antipathy toward the character of Enuo's sister-in-law, Sha, in the story. Enuo loathes Sha to such an extent that she feels a great discomfort when she is alone with her, and even after she and Sha share the same bed in an incestuous encounter with Father-in-Law, there is no improvement in their disharmonious relationship. Instead, the *ménage-a-trois* creates even more jealousy and covert contention, with the result that they never again consent to have intercourse together with Father-in-Law, but insist on seeing him only when the other is not present.

Madam Hibiscus was also antagonistic toward Sha. In the story, when Father-in-law is about to force himself on Sha, and when he is already fondling her breasts, Sha offers no more than token resistance, "taking water from the basin and splashing it onto his face." Madam Hibiscus comments, "Splashing his face with water shows that she is already interested. Why, therefore should she strike such a pose of innocence?!"

It should be noted that from the beginning to the end of her narrative, Madam Hibiscus does not comment in her own voice on the actions of her characters. The commentary, inserted interlineally, is attributed to yet a different person whose pseudonym, "Qingchizi," means "one dominated by passion," and whose name appears next to that of Madame Hibiscus on the title page of the novella. This above-mentioned criticism of Sha, the only comment made by the authoress herself in the entire story, is therefore very unusual and is of particular significance. It demonstrates unmistakably that Madam Hibiscus, like her heroine, detested Sha, and her dislike was so lively that she could not control herself. By abandoning here her objective narrative, she gives in to her feelings, and in so-doing, drops her mask. Her anonymity becomes less important than her need to castigate her sister-in-law.

Outside of the scanty information provided by the autobiographical account in the story, we have no information about the identity of the mysterious Madame Hibiscus. We can only make an educated guess about her background. If she is indeed identical to the heroine of the story, she was probably a native of Hebei province,[52] and moved to settle, as is indicated by

---

52 We cannot exclude the possibility that the author was a native of the present-day Zhejiang province as one scholar has suggested. This seems less likely, however, since the tutor in the story, Gu Deyin, was from Zhaoge county (in present-day Henan province and very close to Hebei province), and it would have been virtually impossible for her to hire someone from so far away to tutor her son if she had lived in the Jiangnan area. The neighbors on her street, moreover, were quite familiar with the name of Zhaoge (see the song they sang when

the first sentence of the story "in a dilapidated town of Zheng-Wei," in the province of Henan in her later years.[53] Her father was a learned scholar, and her mother could at least read and write.[54] Judging from the change of her surname from "Tang" to "Shangguan" after she had been expelled by her husband, we might assume that that she was descended from an old and distinguished clan,[55] and this assumption can help explain why she was able to marry into a wealthy family, even though her father was unlikely to have had much money of his own.

Since she was over seventy when she began to write her memoirs, we can also infer that she was basically a personage of the sixteenth-century, or to be more precise, was probably born in the decade after 1510 (the Zhengde reign), and lived into the Wanli reign (1572–1619). This supposition is further supported by the intertexual time frame in which the story was written. At the beginning of the second part, where the incestuous episode occurs, we find Father-in-Law quoting a couplet that Empress Wu improvised for her husband-to-be: "How fortunate that before even in the brocade tent we meet / I have sprinklings of dew from the golden basin received." Since this two-line verse is from *Lord of Perfect Satisfaction*, it sets an upper limit on the dating of *Memoir of a Crazy Old Woman*. It cannot have been published earlier than the mid-sixteenth century. Since the Prefaces of both *Dongxi Jin yanyi* (Romance of the Eastern and Western Jin Dynasties), which was published in 1612, and *The Carnal Prayer Mat*, which was published in 1657, mention the title, it was known to other authors as early as 1612. The fact that it is also mentioned by the author of the much better-known *Prayer Mat* suggests that it had some influence on late erotic works.

Some scholars have claimed that because this novella does not show the slightest influence from *The Plum in the Golden Vase*, it must have been antecedent to it.[56] In other words, it must have appeared between *Lord of*

---

they had heard about her scandal), and judging from this, we have reason to believe that the author lived in a place that was quite close to Zhaoge county.

53 It was likely that, sometime after her divorce, Enuo married Gu Deyin, her lover, and moved to live with him in Zhaoge county, where he was originally from. That is the reason why she used the name Yan Qiongke to suggest her "immigrant" status in Zheng-Wei. Zheng-Wei, where Zhaoge is located, is both a geographical name and a metaphor for the place noted for lewdness in ancient times.

54 See Ko, D. and Mann, S, *op. cit.*

55 The author told us in her story that her family had house slaves and the garden featured a winding veranda, both of which indicate that her family was very wealthy.

56 See, for example, Li Shiren, "*Chipozi: sibainian qian de yibi rensheng canhui lu*" (*Memoir of a Crazy Old Woman*: a Four-Hundred-Year-Old Confession), in *Zhongguo jinhui xiaoshuo manhua* (Informal Discourses on Banned Books in China), ed., Li Shiren, et al., p. 394.

Perfect Satisfaction and *The Plum in the Golden Vase*, whose circulation among the literati class began as early as the 1590s.[57] But how much earlier was it than *The Plum in the Golden Vase*? It seems certain that it was written in the reign of the emperor Shizong (r. 1522–1566) not in that of emperor Shengzong (r. 1572–1619). The two rulers were very different in their tastes, and are known to have influenced the tone of the literature produced during their reigns. Shizong was Daoist by temperament, and it is therefore no accident that *Lord of Perfect Satisfaction* concludes not with retribution for sins of the flesh, but with an ascension to Taoist immortality. Shengzong, on the other hand, was a fervent promoter of Buddhism and Buddhist values. Thus, the fact that *Crazy Old Woman* ends in retribution and repentance, makes it highly likely that the work was published during his *Wanli* reign.[58]

We may further refine the time of publication by quoting another piece of evidence from the preface to *The Plum in the Golden Vase*. This preface, written by the author of the novel himself in the early 1590s, mentioned a number of "romantic" literary oeuvres, including *Lord of Perfect Satisfaction*, which, according to him, was a work by a prominent writer from a "previous generation,"[59] but he makes no mention whatsoever of *Memoir of a Crazy Old Woman*. Does this mean that he had not seen the work, or that the work was contemporary to his own time and not of a "previous generation?" Whichever the case, his testimony helps to verify that the composition of *Memoir of a Crazy Old Woman* was close in time to his own preface, and we thus surmise that it appeared in the decade of the 1580s.[60]

As a late sixteenth-century work, *Memoir of a Crazy Old Woman* has in recent years garnered a good deal of attention for its candid sexual descriptions, and has been characterized by one well-known Chinese literary critic as an Augustinian confession.[61] True, the *Confessions*, with their sincere

---

57 See Yuan Zhonglang, "Shangzhen," quoted from Shen Defu, *Wanli yehuo bian* (Unofficial Records of the Wanli Reign), *juan* 25.

58 Shengzong's mother was a devout believer in Buddhism and Shengzong was strongly influenced by her. For example, he seldom meted out the death penalty even for severe crimes. See Frederick Mote & Denis Twitchett, eds., *Cambridge History of China: Ming Dynasty 1368–1644, Part I*, chapter 9, "The Lung-chi'ing and Wan-li reigns, 1567–1620) written by Ray Huang, p. 514.

59 See Xinxinzi, preface to *Jin Ping Mei Cihua*. Xinxinzi (Scholar of Delight) was also Xu Wei's pseudonym.

60 We should note that the story, when completed, might have first circulated in the form of manuscript among friends and a small group of people, and it could have taken a few years or even dozens of years before it was formally published.

61 See Li Shiren, ibid., p. 391. Augustine's *Confessions* is largely a philosophical work. If *Memoir of a Crazy Old Woman* is indeed Madam Hibiscus' confessions as is claimed by Li

account of the sins committed by the author when he was young, and of his conversion from pagan heresy to Christianity in his later years, partially supports an analogy to its Chinese counterpart, but we should also acknowledge one major difference. In Madam Hibiscus' work, spirituality is never triumphant over carnality. The conversion of the heroine to "Triratna" after what she sees as her mid-life failures, is something forced upon her by her bitter divorce, and is not an act solely of her own volition. Even when she recollects the excesses and dissipations of her younger days, she expresses not so much as a modicum of repentance. The relating of her personal history, as she says at the outset, is simply an act undertaken to preserve the memory of her "precious" romances at a time when she has "one foot already in the grave." The poem with which her lubricous memoir concludes also offers up, in an implicit manner, the justification that because she was born with "lustful roots from a previous life," is essentially "innocent," and is deserving of pardon. She also reminds us that "more than a handful" of women from younger generations engaged in similar, or even more sensational sexual flings.

The concluding words of *Memoir* cannot but remind us of the ending of another picaresque work of erotic East Asian fiction, *The Life of an Amorous Woman (Koshoku Ichidai Onna),* by the brilliant Japanese poet and novelist, Ihara Saikaku (1642–93).[62] In this immensely popular work which went through six editions between 1686 and 1693, we find a similar narrative structure. A reclusive crone "bent double with age," relates to two young men who wish to learn the ways of love, "the story of her life with all its wanton doings." Like Enuo, she was sexually precocious, experienced her first sexual awakenings through hearing the recitation of court poetry, and at the age of twelve, surrendered her virginity to a low-ranking warrior. Aware of her own beauty and acknowledging her hunger for amatory adventure, she embarks on a downward spiral of dissipation, and with each change of bedfellows sinks lower and lower; from Court attendant to concubine of a provincial lord to high-ranking courtesan to tea-house girl to bath-girl to procuress, and finally to a common streetwalker who can ply her trade only in the dark because of her faded looks. At one point, she finds herself naked on a city bridge at midday, shouting "I want a man! I want a man!"[63] and in spite of her frequent resolve

Shiren, it bears more affinity with Jean Jacque Rousseau's *Confessions* (1782) than with Augustine's work, which, basically consists of prayers to God and is testimonial rather than confessional in nature. It has been recently re-translated by Pulitzer Prize winning writer Garry Wills as *Testimony* (2001). See Garry Wills, *Saint Augustine's Memory* (2002), p. xi.

62 Ihara Saikaku, *The Life of an Amorous Woman and Other Writings* (1963), Edited and translated by Ivan Morris.

63 *Amorous Woman*, p. 164.

to change her ways, confesses eventually to over 10,000 liasons. The use of this conventional number seems an exaggeration, and more believable if just as startling, is the scene in which she visits the Temple of 500 Buddhas and can match her various lovers' faces to each one of the different images there! Frequently throughout the story she laments the unfairness of a life where men can do as they wish while women are condemned to drudgery and discrimination, and after her conversion, she concludes her tale with a self-justification not so far from that of Enuo: "I may have lived in this world by selling my body, but is my heart itself polluted?"

In spite of these similarities, and leaving aside the radical differences in social context, the two stories are far apart on the spectrum of erotica. Saikaku is never graphic. His lovers "disport themselves," or "share a pillow," and there is no sense that their love-making is anything but conventional. Saikaku, like his contemporary William Defoe in *Moll Flanders,* is just as concerned with money as with love, though in Japan, unlike England, prudery had not yet been discovered and as a consequence, the penitential characteristics of Defoe are muted in all of Saikaku's work. The unnamed protagonist of *Amorous Woman* conveys no lubricity or lewdness in her sexual encounters, treats each one as a transaction, and moves on to the next without guilt or shame, and with little self-examination. There is no essential difference here between her and Konosuke, the protagonist of Saikaku's *The Life of an Amorous Man (Koshoku Ichidai Otoko).*[64] Both are "masculine" in sexual posture and in their inability to explore the psychological depth of female sexual response, as well as in the absence of self-recrimination we find in *Memoir*. The eroticism here is instead more similar to that of *Lord* than it is to *Memoir*–a clear indication of the female authorship of the latter.

Saikaku's work was not considered pornographic in his lifetime, but it spawned a host of imitators whose sole purpose seemed to be to sensationalize lewdness. If the hallmark of pornography is, as in today's law, a work "without redeeming social value," these works are pornographic. Saikaku, unlike Defoe, does not justify the more lubricious aspects of his work by repeatedly pointing to its moral intent, but he still ends his story on an ambivalent moral note. His heroine, motivated as she has been in her life by sensuality and money, becomes a Buddhist, gives herself up to reciting the Holy Name day and night, and abandons the world to become a pious recluse. She does so, however, not so much to obtain salvation but because the world has nothing left to offer her.

---

[64] Ihara Saikaku, *The Life of an Amorous Man*, trans. Kengi Hamada, Tuttle, (1963).

In *Memoir*, on the other hand, Enuo's repentance is genuine. She enumerates each of her sins, bites her fingers in penance, and resolves to sin no more.

There are, of course, values beyond morality which elevate a work beyond mere pornography and render them worthy of translation and dissemination. *Lord*, for instance, is a landmark in Chinese literary history as the first to push erotic literature beyond anything previously seen, and is notable for dealing with themes unprecedented in historical fiction. It presents the joys of sensual pleasure, especially female pleasure, without demanding repentance. *Memoir* is equally graphic in depicting the act of coitus, but also explores the psychological depths of the female sexual experience, as well as the familial and social *mores* of the late-Ming, and the condition of the women who inhabited that world.

It is also a work of literary value.

It should be noted, first of all, that in the literature of dynastic China, works of autobiography, particularly those related to one's private or sexual life, are extremely rare. The best-known example, and the only one known to the non-specialist, is Shen Fu's *Fusheng liuji* (Six Chapters of My Floating Life), published much later in the heyday of the Qing dynasty. Madame Hibiscus is thus also an innovator in this genre; and her work is perhaps the first in all of Chinese literature to employ such techniques as first-person narration and "flashbacks," in relating her boudoir experiences.

These narrative innovations have gone largely unnoticed, overshadowed as they are by the graphic accounts of her premarital and extramarital affairs. Even in her own time, if we accept that hers is a true autobiography, these affairs were successfully hidden from her family and from others in her immediate circle. When her husband, for example, casts her off and sends her back to her parents' home because of her affair with the tutor Gu Deyin, he still remains oblivious to the fact that she has had intimate relations not only with the tutor, but also with eleven other men! In the story, all of her sexual encounters, both conventional and unconventional, are recounted in minute detail, but she successfully hides them from prying eyes. From her first taste of "clouds and rain" with her cousin, to her seduction of various household slaves, to such scandalous secrets as her rape by Elder brother-in-law and her incestuous involvement with Father-in-law,[65] no one close to her is any the wiser. The successful concealment of her sexual experiences is another factor

65 With its unabashed sexual openness, Madam Hibiscus' memoir can be compared, to a certain extent, with the recently published autobiography, *The Sexual Life of Catherine M.* by the French writer Catherine Millet (2001).

leading later commentators to focus on her affairs rather than on her narrative skills.

The modern reader might find the story's greatest interest not in the somewhat repetitive incidents of her sexual saga, but in the psychological dimensions of her joyful discovery of sensual pleasure. As we read of a girl in her early teens exploring the forbidden erotic poetry of the *Classic of Odes*, seeking the advice of an older married woman about the mysteries of love and love-making, and then disregarding the advice to avoid tasting of the forbidden fruit, we are struck by the naivete and honesty of her disclosure of her innermost thoughts. Her first forays into the realm of sexual activity are so precious to her, and so deeply imprinted in her psyche that she feels compelled to reveal them. Speaking as Yan Qiongke at the end of her recollections, she says that her first and subsequent sexual experiences "would not have been known to anyone else" had she not felt the necessity to expose them in her memoir.[66] For this reason, the novella is a valuable piece in Chinese literary history not just because of its autobiographical nature, or its narrative innovations. As the work of a female author, it offers us a perspective on themes of emotion, libido, and licentiousness which no male author could provide.

In the late 1920s, a woman writer known by her penname Ding Ling (1904–1986) published an autobiographic novella entitled *Shafei nushi de riji* (Miss Sophia's Diary) which was praised by her contemporaries for its courageous exposé of her three-way relationship with two men.[67] Her heroine, however, is but a pale reflection of Enuo, since her amatory fantasies and experiences are confined to romantic kisses and embraces, and more than anything else, the notoriety of the work reveals how easily shocked were her readers. They had not been familiar with the fleshy exploits of Madame Hibiscus whose fictional heroine has her first precocious experiences before the age of fifteen, and from the time of her marriage into the respectable Luan household, embarks upon a career of adultery exploring, with some relish, a

---

66 In the erotic literature that we have read, none, except for the short story "Tennessee" by Pat Williams (see *Herotica 3*, ed. Susie Bright, pp. 22–37), can be compared with *Memoir of a Crazy Old Woman* for its verisimilitude and emotional strength in presenting a teenage girl's vague yearning for sex, her naïve amatory experiences, and her genuine feelings of infatuation in love.

67 In her real life Ding Ling had a triangular relationship with Hu Yeping (1905–1931) and Shen Congwen (1902–1988), and *Miss Sophia's Diary* was largely based upon her personal experiences. For more information of the relationship of Ding Ling with her lovers, see C. T. Hsia, *A History of Modern Chinese Fiction* (1999), pp. 262–268.

very wide variety of sensual pursuits from shameless seduction to group sex, incest, and unconventional positions in sexual intercourse.[68]

Interestingly enough, when Enuo reviews her life and compares it to that of other indulgent women, she finds nothing very extraordinary in her "misconduct." "More than a handful of beautiful women nowadays engage in romances," she sighs, concluding her reminiscences by reminding her readers of the general condition of debauchery and decadence in the late Ming period. The extent of her libertinism, and her frank pride in it, may surprise even modern readers who have been baptized by the sexual revolution in the West.

Memoir of a Crazy Old Woman, however graphic, also exhibits a distinctly feminine quality which sets it apart from the many erotic stories penned by males in the same time period.[69] In most late-Ming pornographic works, male authors dwell upon little more than the appearance of genitalia and the act of coitus; and more often than not, engage in exaggerations around male size and stamina, and female response. Works like *The Embroidered Couch*, and *The Carnal Prayer Mat*, much better-known than *Memoir of a Crazy Old Woman*, are typical; and *Lord of Perfect Satisfaction*, translated here, is another good example. *Memoir*, on the other hand, depicts the sexual act in a relatively realistic fashion, devoid of excessive prurience and overstatement. In the story we find that a lover's phallus may be as large as that of a donkey, but from time to time, it becomes fatigued, and is unable to perform its nocturnal duty until it has been nursed back to strength on *yang*-strengthening tonics. Here too, we find that the rapture of sexual congress can sometimes propel a woman into a state of delirium, but just as often, intercourse fails to arouse her to climax, and on some occasions even hurts her. The story thus presents the world of a female sexuality and amorous engagement in a way that is both authentic and natural, and it is filled with the sort of finely-executed details rarely found in the works by male authors. With raunchiness and hyperbole largely absent, the story is more erotic than pornographic.

In describing the life of a woman prone to yield to her lust and wantonness, the story is also "feminine" in the sense that it portrays a wider

---

68 This is simply a historical comparison, not an artistic judgment on Ding Ling's *Miss Sophia's Diary*, which, obviously, has its own merits. For a comprehensive discussion of Ding Ling's works, *Miss Sophia's Diary* included, see Yi-tsi Mei Feuerwerker, *Ding Ling's Fiction: Ideology and Narrative in Modern Chinese Literature* (1982).

69 Simone de Beauvoir, in *The Second Sex*, takes the position that a woman's sexuality is intrinsically different from a man's. "Her eroticism, and therefore her sexual world have a special form of their own and therefore cannot fail to engender a sensuality, a sensitivity, of a special nature." Quoted from *Erotic Stories by Women*, eds. Richard Glyn Jones & A. Susan Williams, Introduction, Penguin (1995), p. ix.

range of female emotion, passion, and love than is found, for instance, in *Lord of Perfect Satisfaction*. Here we seem to be observing the heroine in the round, experiencing not only her lechery and intemperance, but also her feelings, her yearnings, and her sentimentality. Yes, Enuo seems dedicated to the search for her own pleasure, and to "zipless" sexual satisfaction with a parade of men, but she can also fall helplessly in love.

Her cousin, Huimin is the first to win her love, and the poem she composes to proclaim her profound love is genuinely touching. When he is forced to return home, she confesses that she misses him so much that she weeps every night, and is scarcely able to "sleep a wink." She also falls in love with Xiangchan, a handsome young actor; but her love this time is not based on his sexual prowess. She is enraptured by his physical beauty, which she compares favorably to that of "a lady fair." He is not, however, a virile lover, and in fact, his endowment is so small that she can barely feel it inside her, and she receives little stimulation or pleasure from intercourse with him. In spite of the disappointing sex, however, she dotes upon him: "Your beauty is a feast for my eyes," she says to him, "and I feel I am too ugly to be your match. I insisted that we make love only in the hope that we would never forget each other afterwards."

To be sure, we cannot stretch the point that there is in Enuo more love than lust.[70] A man like Datu, who fails to arouse her emotionally, is intolerable to her, but so too, is a man like Ketao, whose virility and stamina do not meet her sexual standards. What she really desires is an ideal combination of gentlemanly tenderness and gratifying sexual performance, and it is only when she meets her son's tutor that she finds this ideal combination. Unlike lesser works of erotica published in the late Ming, *Memoir* is not a monochromatic picture of sex for the sake of sex. The author, perhaps due to her feminine sensibility, juxtaposes love and sex with balance and nuance.

Commenting on this story in his classic catalogue *Riben Dongjing suojian tongsu xiaoshuo shumu* (Bibliography of Popular Chinese Fiction preserved in Tokyo, Japan), the late scholar of Ming-Qing fiction, Sun Kaidi (1902–1992) contends that the work is "a masterpiece [in the literature] of the 'northern community'" (*beili zhi xiong*),[71] the term "northern community" referring to the area of prostitution and hence pornography. Patrick Hanan, the translator of

---

70 For a detailed discussion of the concepts of love and lust, see Huang, M., *Desire and Fictional Narrative in Late Imperial China*, Harvard U.P. (2001).

71 See *Riben Dongjing suojian Zhongguo tongsu xiaoshuo shumu*, p. 165. This comment has been deleted in Sun's revised version *Zhongguo tongsu xiaoshuo shumu* (Bibliography of Chinese Popular Fiction).

Carnal Prayer Mat, expressed a similar opinion in his conversation with the authors some years ago, suggesting that its significance has long been ignored.[72]

We have commented above on several features of *Memoir of a Crazy Old Woman*: its autobiographical realism, its extravagant and audacious lasciviousness, and its distinctively feminine mode of presentation.[73] There are other dimensions of the narrative which make it an important work, but we would like to raise only one more.

Previous commentators in China have universally failed to make any mention of the sophisticated social message embedded in the story, a message lacking in all the lesser erotic works of the period. Sex in this story is not depicted as the isolated activity of consenting partners in the bedroom, but is presented in the context of the community and most particularly, of the family. When Enuo, at an early age, experiences an adolescent curiosity about sexual matters, the author attributes it to her scholarly family background. She was taught not only the rudiments of reading and writing, but was introduced to the *Classic of Poetry*, and allowed to explore even those sections considered unsuitable for young women. Madame Hibiscus comments further on the permissive atmosphere of her upbringing—her father's homosexual relations with the son of a household slave, her mother's leniency in disciplining her daughter, and her female neighbor's "instruction" on the delights of lovemaking—all these factors contributed to her willingness to flout the prohibitions of society and to make the ill-considered decision to sleep with her cousin, and thus sacrifice her virginity before she was married. Her new husband's family, with its wealth and nobility, its magnificent mansions, and its lush gardens with serpentine verandas, seems to resemble the prosperity and lavishness of the manor *Daguanyuan* in the later novel, *Honglou meng* (Dream of the Red Mansion), but inside its seemingly decorous compound, nearly every male, from her father-in-law to her brothers-in-law, "scratched in the ashes" (*pahui*),[74] in unscrupulous incest. Surrounded by kinfolk like these, how could Enuo have distanced herself from their contamination and preserved her own purity even if she had wished to do so?

---

72 Patrick Hanan's paper on six Chinese erotic novels entitled "The Erotic Novel: Some Early Reflections", which was presented at an Indiana Conference in 1983, has never been published.

73 In most erotic stories written by men, women are presented simply as an object of men's desire. *Memoir of a Crazy Old Woman*, which is similar in this respect to Pauline Réage's *Story of O*, avoids the language of male sexual discourse and presents female erotic consciousness from a female perspective.

74 A Chinese colloquial expression for incest.

The story, in describing the gradual process of Enuo's "degeneration," thus makes a connection between her voluptuous life and her familial and social circumstances, a connection very rarely presented in such manner in sixteenth-century Chinese fiction. It thereby sheds much light on the *mores* and life-style of the upper levels of society in the later years of the Ming dynasty.

Madam Hibiscus describes Enuo's life in an extended, patriarchal family from the perspective both of an objective narrator and a sympathetic critic of her heroine. Her story of a woman's life, which is filled with love and pleasure, suffering and resentment, is multi-dimensional and replete with irony. She readily defends and forgives the transgressions of Enuo who is, after all, her surrogate self; and one may even detect in the story an element of self-pity. While there is no doubt that Enuo is a loose woman, a seductress, and an unapologetic adulteress, her unwillingness to have intercourse with a man she finds repulsive [75] and her passion for the tutor to whom she is more than willing to devote her life, calls our attention to a different aspect of her psyche–her courageous pursuit of an ideal partner and a happy marriage! This, perhaps, was also the goal of our mysterious author.

In sharp contrast, she exhibits acrimony rather than compassion when she comes to the portrayal of such "close kin" as Father-in-law. Sympathetic as he may seem, since his wife is on medication and unable to provide the conjugal relations he desires, Madame Hibiscus shows him no mercy. The molestation of his daughters-in-law, and his claim that he has a "right" to have sex with them, assaults her sensibilities just as it assaults our own. She makes him even more repugnant toward the conclusion of the story as he, in spite of his attempt to whitewash himself, utters: "My second son, it is your misfortune to have a wife so lewd and unfaithful." In the end, he stands awash in hypocrisy, unmasked as a duplicitous liar.

It is perhaps this social critique in *Memoir of a Crazy Old Woman* which most clearly sets it apart from other erotica of the time. In it, we find an implicit plea for greater personal and sexual freedom for women along with a condemnation both of patriarchal power, and of the iron-clad tradition that a married woman remain forever chaste, and faithful to her marital vows.

Like *Lord of Perfect Satisfaction*, *Memoir of a Crazy Old Woman* was shockingly explicit in its sexual descriptions, and this is the principal reason

---

[75] As Susan William states, "For the most part, it is men rather than women who pay for anonymous or impersonal sex–whatever straight or gay–with those who can be hired on city streets." See *Erotic Stories by Women*, Introduction, p. ix. Enuo's unwillingness to be forced into intercourse with men she dislikes is yet another indication of the author's female sexual sub-consciousness.

for its interdiction in Qing, Republican and post-1949 China. Both novellas remain largely-unknown in China today.

At the same time, the social critique found in *Memoir* makes it a more subversive work, and its narrative style makes it a more innovative landmark in Chinese fiction. Interestingly, one well-known Western scholar of Chinese vernacular literature, claimed in a standard study, that first-person narrative and the technique of flashback was "imported" from Europe to China at the turn of the twentieth century.[76] Clearly, she was unaware that Madame Hibiscus had anticipated this "import" by four centuries! Similarly, when Wei Hui's explicit sexual memoirs, *Shanghai baobei*,[77] became a runaway bestseller and a *cause célèbre* in China some years ago, not a single reviewer and not a single member of the educated public made the obvious connection with *Memoir of a Crazy Old Woman*.

The obscurity of *Memoir* is undeserved.

It is our belief that it is a classic of its genre, and that without it, Chinese literature would be the poorer, and our knowledge both of that literature and the social *milieu* which produced it, would be less complete. As an erotic autobiography of great aesthetic sophistication, it can be enjoyed on many levels, and is one of only a handful of erotic Ming works which is worthy of the test of time.[78]

We present these two novellas in the same volume not so much because they were both products of the sixteenth-century in China, or because both were considered salacious in their own time and by later generations, or because

---

76 "The first-person personal narrative mode is certainly an innovation in the history of Chinese vernacular fiction. Wu Woyao's *Strange Events* is the first occurrence of the first-person narrative in *baihua* literature. Its appearance is especially significant in comparison with occidental literature, where first-person narrative has been well established since classical Greece." Milena Dolezelova-Velingerova, "The Narrative Modes in Late Qing Novels," in Milena Dolezelova-Velingerova, ed., *The Chinese Novel at the Turn of Century* University of Toronto Press (1980), p. 66.

77 In translation, Zhou Weihui, *Shanghai Baby*, Simon and Schuster (2001).

78 What the English translator of *Story of O* says about Pauline Réage's novel is also applicable to *Memoir of a Crazy Old Woman*: "*Story of O* is the work of an original writer, who has dared to present us with certain truths, or intimations of truth, rarely found in literature. However much one may disagree with, or even profoundly dislike, these truths (or, if you will, these ideas), Pauline Réage has done what all good artists aim for and, from the lethargy or our set ways and routine lives, prick us into consciousness, provoke a reaction (whether positive or negative, it matters little) within us; in short, to make us think. That in itself is a rare enough occurrence so that we should be grateful indeed whenever we have the good fortune to encounter it." See *Story of O*, p. xii.

both were composed in elegant literary language (*wenyan*) interlined with some coarse phraselogy. We are interested in a different sort of comparison. Both novellas are focused on the sexual life of woman, and both portray a certain view of femininity in their protagonists–in one case, from the third-person perspective of a male author, and in the other, from the first-person perspective of a female author. Moreover, both espouse a kind of "proto-feminism" in their attempts to portray female sexuality from a female perspective and in their common advocacy of greater freedoms for women in their personal and romantic lives. They perhaps represent the earliest stirrings of female sexual awareness in Chinese literary history.[79] We have arranged the two stories in chronological order despite our personal preference for Madam Hibiscus' memoir and our belief that it is the better work. In whichever order we present them, the common focus on female eroticism is clear.[80] Our most difficult task has been to understand the historical context in which our two authors lived their lives and produced their works.[81] Of one thing we are certain, though. The voices we hear and the pictures we see in these earliest works of Chinese erotica are far different than those to be found in China's orthodox literary canons.

---

79 In the Chinese literary tradition, female expression of sexual pleasure can perhaps be traced back to the female poet Yu Xuanji's (844–871) erotic poems, and prior to that, Empress Wu Zetian's *Shengxian taizi bei* (The Heir-Apparent Ascends to Immortality Inscription), which, according to Qigong, was composed and transcribed by Empress Wu herself, describing how she enjoyed her *mianshou*, Zhang Changzong, who, dressed like an immortal and mounted on a wooden horse, danced for her in the palace. See Qigong, *Lunshu jueju* (Quatrains on Calligraphy), p. 90–91. These poetic works lack the social significance of *Memoir of a Crazy Old Woman*.

80 For one exposition of the feminist approach to literary analysis, see Elaine Showalter, "The Feminist Critical Revolution," in Elaine Showalter, ed., *The New Feminist Criticism: Essays on Women, Literature, and Theory* (1985).

81 The late-Ming has received a good deal of attention from social and intellectual historians in China. Two of the good studies, *Wan-Ming shifeng yu wenxue* (The Mood of Literati and Literature in Late-Ming) by Xia Xianchun and *Wan-Ming sixiang shilun* (Historical Interpretation of Late Ming Thought) by Ji Wenfu, approach this era from different angles, and are very useful in providing us with a better understanding of the social context of late Ming erotica. In English, *The Cambridge History of China* is a good starting-point.

LORD OF PERFECT SATISFACTION

Preface

What is "The Lord of Perfect Satisfaction" about?

It is about Empress Wu Zetian's sexual life. The story may be risqué, yet it is as enlightening as history. Long ago, due to the arrangements of the Marquis of Liu,[1] the Four White-haired Recluses came to the assistance of the Crown Prince and the Han dynasty thereby continued.[2] What a great contribution the Marquis made to his country! Empress Wu Zetian, tyrannical and shamelessly dissipated, deposed the legitimate successor of the Tang and proclaimed herself Emperor, and no one was able to stop her. Had it not been for Aocao's endeavors, notwithstanding that his influence arose through an illicit sexual relationship, the re-enthronement of Zhongzong would have been out of the question. Was not Aocao a man meritorious to his country? Without him, even persons with the ability of the Marquis of Liu or of the Four White-haired Recluses could not have helped restore Zhongzong as Heir Apparent, however hard they racked their brains. "Entering through a window," as *The Book of Changes* says, was precisely the method that Aocao adopted. Thus, though the story may be risqué, is it not as enlightening as history?

A Dismissed Official of Huayang

1 The Marquis of Liu was Zhang Liang (?–186 B.C.E.), who, after helping Liu Bang establish the Han dynasty, was enfeoffed in Liu, or Liucheng, in Xuzhou, where he had first met the emperor.

2 Liu Bang, the founding emperor of the Han dynasty, had intended to depose the Crown Prince, his son by Empress Lu, and to install the Prince of Zhao, his son by his favorite concubine Lady Qi, as heir apparent. The Marquis of Liu, giving in to the entreaties of Empress Lu, sent for the four old recluses of noble character and high prestige, whom Liu Bang respected, and they successfully persuaded him to give up the idea of deposing the Crown Prince. For details, see Sima Qian, *Shiji* (Records of the Grand Historian), vol. 6, pp. 2044–46.

Lord of Perfect Satisfaction[1]

Wu Zetian, the empress of the imperial palace, was the daughter of Wu Shihuo,[2] governor-general of the Jingzhou prefecture. Her childhood-name was Mei-niang.[3] When she was fourteen years old, Emperor Wen[4] heard of her beauty and took her into his harem, conferring upon her the title *Cairen* (consort of the third rank).[5] Long afterwards, the Emperor fell victim to disease. The future emperor, Gaozong,[6] then Heir-Apparent, came into the inner palace to look after him and with all attentiveness fed him decoctions of herbal medicine. Mei-niang was waiting upon the Emperor by his bedside. At the sight of her, Gaozong conceived a deep passion for her and wished to enjoy her favors. Yet a chance did not present itself until he went to the privy, where Mei-niang, after following him in, went down on her knees before him with a golden basin of water held deferentially in her hands. Gaozong teased her by splashing its water upon her, intoning:

---

1 This novella is also known as "A Story of Enjoyment in the Bedchamber" (*Kunyu qing zhuan*).

2 Wu Shihuo (577–635) came from a rich family in Bingzhou and had engaged in the lumber business for many years before serving the future-emperor,Taizong, in his establishment of the Tang dynasty. He was later appointed Minister of the Board of Works. He died at his post as Governor of Jingzhou.

3 "Mei-niang", in Chinese, means "charming or lovely lady." This was a name Emperor Wen [Taizong] gave to Wu Zetian when he selected her as his concubine at the age of fourteen. No historical account mentions her original name, but according to Lei Jiaji, "Wu Yue" might possibly be her original name. For details, see Lei Jiaji, *Wu Zetian zhuan* (Biography of Wu Zetian), chapter 2, pp. 22–32.

4 Emperor Wen, whose name was Li Shimin (r. 627–650), is usually known by his posthumous title, "Taizong."

5 In the Tang dynasty, consorts of the third rank numbered 27, and were called *cairen*, literarily meaning "talented woman."

6 Gaozong, whose name was Li Zhi, occupied the throne from 649 to 683.

Suddenly I feel as if I were on Mount Wu,[7] with a girl of my dreams,
But alas, though within my sight she is yet far beyond my reach.

Mei-niang replied at once by improvising another two lines in the same rhyme:

How fortunate that before even in the brocade tent we meet,
I have sprinkles of dew[8] from the golden basin received.

Gaozong was greatly delighted, and led her, hand in hand, to an empty room inside the palace, where they engaged in sexual congress until both of them, in tender affection, had tasted immense pleasure. After having finished, Mei-niang held on to Gaozong's clothes, sobbing: "Although I am a low-ranking concubine," she said, "I have long been serving His Majesty. Now to fulfill the wish of Your Highness, I have violated the statute against illicit fornication. I don't know, My Lord, when you are enthroned, how you will treat me."

Gaozong undid the translucent, nine-dragon jade buckle from his belt and gave it to her. "Upon my accession," he said, "I will make you my empress!"

Mei-niang bowed twice and took it. From that time onward they would make love whenever Gaozong came in to attend the moribund Emperor.

On his deathbed, the emperor had Mei-niang sent to the Ganye Temple,[9] where, as had been the custom, she shaved her head and entered Buddhist orders as a nun. After his enthronement Gaozong went to the Ganye Temple to burn incense and privately told Mei-niang to grow her hair. When her hair grew seven feet long, he summoned her back into the imperial harem, conferring upon her the title of *Zhaoyi* (consort of second rank).

After her return to the palace, Lady Wu entered immediately upon a rivalry with [the reigning] Empress Wang as well as with the concubine Xiao Shufei[10] for the Emperor's favor. That year she was thirty-two years old.

"Your Majesty is on the throne now," she said sobbing to Gaozong, "Don't you remember what you promised me when you gave me the buckle of your belt?"

Gaozong considered the idea seriously and began to estrange himself from both the Empress and Xiao Shufei. Finally he decided to dethrone the

---

7 Mount Wu is a metaphor for a trysting place.

8 A euphemism for the ejaculation of semen.

9 Ganye Temple was also called Anye Temple. See Wang Diwu, *Wu Zetian shidai* (The Era of Wu Zetian), p. 73.

10 Her name was Xiao Liangdi. In the Tang dynasty, Shufei, together with Guifei, Defei, and Xianfei, were consorts of the highest rank, just below that of the empress.

Empress and replace her by Lady Wu. The next day, at the morning audience, he told Changsun Wuji[11] of his intention.

"Empress Wang is childless whereas Lady Wu has sons," said the emperor. "I am planning to remove the empress and install Lady Wu in her place. What do you think?"

Wuji dared not utter a word, but an elder statesman standing close to the throne, whose name was Chu Suiliang,[12] made so bold as to offer his opinion: "Empress Wang was crowned in the grand coronation ceremony. Our late Emperor, before his death, held Your Majesty's hand as he spoke to me and other ministers, saying: 'I am entrusting my good son and my good daughter-in-law to your care.' His words still ring in my ears, and I dare not forget them. Empress Wang has not committed any crime and there is no reason to demote her. If Your Majesty really wishes to replace her with someone else, please select from one of the most distinguished aristocratic clans in the land. Lady Wu served [i.e. was a concubine of] our late emperor and then entered a Buddhist temple as a nun. This has been known to everyone and there is no way of covering it up. As a humble servant, I should not give Your Majesty counsel against your will. I deserve the death penalty for my offence."

Having so said, he removed his official cap and knocked his head violently on the stair until his forehead bled. "I am returning my ivory tablet[13] to Your Majesty," he said. "Pray permit me to go back to my native village."

Lady Wu, hidden behind the screen, heard every word Chu Suiliang had said. She roared ferociously, "Why not flog this sharp-tongued traitor until he is dead!"

Furious, Gaozong put Chu Suiliang immediately to the cruelest torture, which swiftly ended his life.[14] Changsun Wuji was then demoted to the

---

11 Changsun Wuji (?–659), a native of Luoyang in Henan province, was emperor Taizong's brother-in-law. In the palace coup which helped Taizong destroy his brothers and seize the throne Wuji was his most important supporter. He was rewarded with the highest official posts during Taizong's reign, and was appointed *taiwei* (official of first rank) when Gaozong ascended the throne. He was the "elder statesman" and the most influential official in the early reign of Gaozong. Chinese emperors, though above the law, were forbidden by long tradition to depose an empress unless she had engaged in treasonous activity, or unless the emperor had very strong support from his highest civil officials.

12 Chu Suiliang (596–658) was a high-ranking official in Taizong's reign, and after Gaozong's enthronement, was appointed Prime Minister. He gained additional prestige for his superb calligraphy.

13 This is another way of saying, "I intend to resign." In imperial China officials were obliged to hold a tablet in a long, narrow shape, usually made of ivory or jade, when attending meetings at court. The ivory tablet therefore became a token of the tenure of one's official position.

prefecture of Tanzhou as governor-general.[15] A historian of later times, upon reading of this incident, composed the following poem:

Lord, how loyal you were as a minister,
And how selfless your word of advice!
How can we find your valor so upright,
Elsewhere but in Bi Gan the advisor?[16]
Your heart changed not its color of blood,
Even when you were about to resign.
Hitting your forehead on the royal flight,
You were shedding red rivulets of flood.
Oh, the dominance of the relentless phoenix,[17]
Silenced all who dared to speak with no fear.
Incestuous relations[18] *she enjoyed for years*
Muddling the emperor by words from her lips.
But sage rulers were on the throne finally,[19]
Rehabilitating you with overdue respect;
Your devoted heart was then at long rest set,
Appreciated by all heartily.

With Chu Suiliang sentenced to death and Changsun Wuji banished to a distant provincial post, no one else dared to voice his [contrary] opinions. Lady Wu was then enthroned as Empress.

Now on the throne, Empress Wu was willful and unbridled. She presided over the court as equal partner with her husband Gaozong, overstepping her authority and wreaking tremendous havoc on the imperial regalia. Gaozong showed great favor to her and was also very much afraid of her. People therefore called them "twin sovereigns."

---

14 According to the official Tang history, Chu Suiliang was not immediately tortured and executed. He was only demoted at that time.

15 The official history of the Tang tells us that it was Chu Suiliang, instead of Changsun Wuji, who was demoted to the prefecture of Tanzhou as governor-general. Changsun Wuji was demoted to Qianzhou, where he died of illness.

16 Bi Gan was the uncle of the tyrannical king Zou (r. 11th century, B.C.E.). Despite great risks, he frequently offered admonitions against the king's actions and was finally executed.

17 Empress Wu. Emperors were symbolized by the dragon and empresses by the Chinese phoenix.

18 Emperor Wen (Taizong) and Emperor Gaozong were father and son, and Wu Zetian had sexual relations with both of them.

19 "Sage rulers" refer to the later emperors of the Tang dynasty such as Zhongzong (r. 705–710), Dezong (r. 780–785), and Wenzong (r. 826–841). Zhongzong transferred Chu Suiliang's exiled family back to the capital when he was on the throne, Dezong bestowed upon him a posthumous title, and Wenzong appointed his descendents to important official positions.

Later, suffering from dizziness and impaired vision, Gaozong was unable to write instructions on the memorials submitted to the throne, so he very often had to rely on Empress Wu in reading reports and making decisions for him. The empress was by nature intelligent, learned and widely read in history and literature. She was capable of handling matters to his taste most of the time.

She then favricated a case against the former Empress Wang and the concubine Xiao [Shufei] and after convicting them of alleged crimes, had each of them flogged with two hundred strokes, cut off their hands and feet, and threw them into a wine vat. After they had been thoroughly wine-saturated, she had their corpses dismembered and buried in the rear courtyard.[20]

After her enthronement, Empress Wu ennobled her father, Wu Shihuo, as the Marquis of Zhou, and later bestowed upon him the title, Prince of Taiyuan.[21]

When Gaozong passed away, Heir Apparent Li Zhe,[22] posthumously titled Zhongzong, ascended the throne. He installed his principal consort, née Wei, as his empress. Yet his reign did not last long, and in the fifth year of his sovereignty[23] he was suddenly set aside by Empress Wu[24] as Prince of Luling. His younger brother, Li Dan,[25] was then designated to replace him, but was allowed to reign only in name. After seven years of his nominal rule, Empress Wu demoted Li Dan to [the title of] "Emperor Expectant" and proclaimed herself "Peerless Empress." She built seven temples to her appropriately-titled ancestors, and soon afterwards dispatched troops to kill the Prince of Langya, Li Chong and the Prince of Yue, Li Zhen, and had the Tang royal clan slaughtered. She re-named herself Wu Zhao,[26] called her reigning dynasty

---

20 This incident is true, and is probably cited here to show the ruthlessness and cruelty of the empress as she took revenge on former rivals who were no longer a threat to her position.

21 When Wu Zetian reigned as Emperor, she bestowed upon her late father many other grandiose titles. After overthrowing the Tang dynasty in 690, Empress Wu chose "Zhou" as the name for her new dynasty, both to honor her father, and to echo the name of China's longest dynasty (1027–221 B.C.E.) which was also revered as the era of Confucius.

22 Li Zhe, or Li Xian, was Gaozong's seventh son and Empress Wu's third son.

23 Li Zhe was the empress' third son. She is said by hostile historians to have murdered her eldest son who openly criticized her, and to have executed her second son who was similarly disloyal, on a trumped-up charge of treason.

24 In the original Chinese text the words *taihou* ("empress dowager") and the word *hou* ("empress") are used interchangeably after the enthronement of Li Zhe. In the translation, we refer to her as "Empress Wu" or "the empress" for the sake of clarity.

25 Li Dan was the fourth son of Empress Wu.

26 The character *zhao* consists of two parts; the top part meaning "bright" and the bottom part meaning " void or sky." It was a new character created by the empress herself, and at

Zhou, and gave herself a grandiose new title: "Peerless, Holy Emperor, Golden Wheel" [27]

She was attempting to appoint her nephew Wu Sansi as Heir Apparent when Prime Minister Di Renjie[28] remonstrated.

"Your Majesty," wrote Di Renjie diplomatically, "there is a problem in your appointment of Wu Sansi as Heir Apparent. After the cessation of your life, your nephew would ascend the throne. Yet since Your Majesty is his aunt, how can he erect a monument in your memory in *his* ancestestral temple?"[29]

After reading this memorial Empress Wu set up Li Dan as Emperor instead, but she made him adopt her surname, Wu. This raised much opposition from people who were anxious to topple the Zhou House and re-establish the Tang royal lineage. But,

With the parrot's[30] dream shattered thanks to Di's advice,
Back on the throne was her young son from high skies.[31]

Empress Wu knew that because she was a notorious adulteress, the populace was reluctant to accept her, [32] and she was therefore relentless in the suppression [of potential enemies]. Those falsely accused by her of staging armed rebellions, and thereafter condemned to death were numerous. Indeed she was a ruler both of easy virtue and of cold-blooded cruelty. A historian of later times satirized her in the following poem:

---

the same time, she created more than a dozen new characters and decreed that they replace existing words. The measure was meant to display her erudition and to invite comparison with the legendary and revered inventor of Chinese script. Her new characters can be seen today on documents and inscriptions of the period, though they were banned from the Tang restoration onward.

27 Wu Zetian was the only female in Chinese history to call herself "emperor," and it was said that she often dressed in male attire as she presided over the court or attended grand ceremonials. After her death, her son, Zhongzong, changed her title back to "empress."

28 Di Renjie (607–700) was a capable and upright official renowned especially for his courage in remonstrating with Empress Wu. He was also known as Judge Di, and is a well-known protagonist in numerous *gong'an* novels, many of which have been adapted and translated into English by the renowned sinologist, Robert van Gulik.

29 Ancestral temples honored only the direct line of descent.

30 "Parrot" refers to Empress Wu, Wu Sansi, since in Chinese "parrot" (pronounced *wu*) is homophonous with the surname Wu. Empress had hoped his nephew would become her successor.

31 "High skies" is a metaphor for the distant place to which the Heir Apparent was banished.

32 This, of course, is the author's own conjecture, based perhaps on works written about the empress between her own time and his own. The empress was never technically an adulteress since her notorious affairs all took place after the death of her husband.

A hen crowing in the vacated Purple Mansion,[33]
Showered flowers crimson;[34]
On the throne sat a woman,
Who drove the Emperor to the Eastern Section.[35]
She and the Zhangs[36] *enjoyed their intimacy,*
Restoring order was left to Lord Di.[37]
Yet the coup d'état had been foreseen,
Even today, we revere Li Chunfeng in memory.[38]

Since the empress placed her reliance on the Zhang brothers and employed evil minions like Lai Junchen and Suo Yuanli in carrying out her unlawful orders, no officials dared to offer their admonitions. Had it not been for Di Renjie's effective remedies, the affairs of state would no doubt have fallen into a disastrous state of ruin, and the empress would have had no time for sexual enjoyment with a newly-introduced man named Xue Aocao,[39] whose intriguing story is well worth relating.

Back at the end of the Sui dynasty (589–618), Xue Ju called out his troops in revolt in Longxi and proclaimed himself Emperor of Qin. His second son Xue Renjing,[40] together with his elder brother Xue Rengao, was defeated in a

---

33 The Purple Mansion (*zichen dian*) was a building in the inner sanctum of the imperial palace in Luoyang, where Empress Wu often did her routine work. See Sima Guang, *Zizhi tongjian* (Comprehensive Mirror for Aid in Government, vol. 14, p. 6419.

34 This simile refers to Empress Wu's bloody suppression of all dissidents. "Jishu" (several trees) in the original Chinese text is obviously a mistake; it should be "jishu" (a tree with a chicken roosting on it). For its allusion, see *Xin Tang shu* (New History of the Tang), vol. 11, p. 3483.

35 Eastern Section (*donggong*), i.e., the east wing of the palace, was where the Heir Apparent, not the emperor, resided.

36 The Zhangs refer to the two Zhang brothers, Zhang Changzong (?–705) and Zhang Yizhi (?–705), both of whom became Empress Wu's favorites, and perhaps lovers, in her last years. Their unrestrained corruption and interference in state matters was one cause of her forced abdication. They were murdered in 705 by a group of restoration officials, while they attended one of the empress' parties. Devastated by their fate, she abdicated.

37 The Prime Minister Di Renjie. Cf. note 29.

38 Li Chunfeng (602–670) was a Daoist seer and Tang loyalist who predicted both the usurpation and the restoration.

39 Xue Aocao is a fictitious character, of whom there are no records in either official or unofficial histories. He is largely based upon the historical figure Xue Huaiyi, who later appears himself in this story. This is an interesting literary device. See the Introduction of this work for further information on Huaiyi.

40 Xue Renjing is a fictitious character. *Xin Tangshu* (New History of the Tang) only mentions two sons of Xue Ju (?-618), the elder son Xue Rengao and the younger son Xue Renyue. See *Xin Tangshu*, vol. 12, pp. 3705–3708.

battle at the Shallow Waters,[41] and after his surrender, was executed in Chang'an.

Renjing's favorite concubine Suji had previously had a liaison with their house servant and had just become pregnant. After having been expelled in a fury by Renjing, she went to live at the Six Waters, and when Renjing was defeated and executed, she alone escaped. She gave birth to a son called Yufeng.

Yufeng, when grown up, was very fond of reading *Master Sun's Art of War*[42] and also the *Wu Qi*.[43] Due to his family's calamity, however, he had no intention of pursuing an official career. He married in Cao and had two sons, the elder one named Xue Boying and the younger one, Xue Aocao. In the third year of the Yifeng reign (678) when Gaozong was on the throne, Yufeng passed away and Aocao and his elder brother moved to settle in Chang'an. But in the first year of the Yonglong reign (680) Boying died also. Aocao then traveled to Luoyang, and there he sojourned. That year he was eighteen years old.

A man of seven feet in height,[44] Aocao was light-skinned and handsome, with finely chiseled facial features. His arms were strong and muscular and his strides were agile and vigorous. He not only had extensive knowledge of the classics and history, but was good at calligraphy, painting, musical instruments and chess as well. Since he had a great capacity for liquor, he also often went on chivalrous adventures.

He had a huge member, the prodigious size of which verged upon abnormality. Having heard of its reputation, nosy young men in his neighborhood would invite him to drink if they ran into him on street, and would then beg him to display it for their amusement.

"I am encumbered with such a large object and have yet to taste its carnal delight," Aocao would reply. "Since I can't even put it to use for myself, how then can it provide you fellows with pleasure?"

On their insistence, however, Aocao would produce his member, which, in full display, revealed the luxuriance of a ridged and colossal tree-trunk. There were four or five indentations around its covered head, and as the

---

41 Shallow Waters (Qianshui, or Qianshui yuan) are in present-day Gansu province, in the remote northwest.

42 *Master Sun's Art of War* (Sunzi bingfa) is a work on military affairs by the famous strategist Sun Bin, a contemporary of Mencius (372–289 B.C.E.).

43 *Wu Qi* is also a book on military affairs by the famous strategist Wu Qi (?–381 B.C.E.). The work is now lost.

44 The Chinese foot is smaller than our own. Aocao was probably over six feet tall, unusual for that period of history.

gristle arose in feverish excitement, the flesh protruded slowly as if a snail was emerging from its shell. From its head to its base, twenty odd veins and ridges jutted out like earthworms, so lustrous and shiny that they could be perceived even in a dark cave. This [shining newness] occurred because it had never been immersed in female fluids.

Astonished upon seeing it, the viewers would try to hang on the top end of his erection a bag containing a peck of grain, and Aocao's ability to bear the weight with little difficulty would make them all convulse with laughter.

Someone once took him to a brothel. The courtesans there all became very excited as they saw a beautiful young man coming in for a visit. They drank with him while singing and playing games of chance and there were none who did not take a fancy to him. However, as Aocao undressed and exposed that object of his to them, they all fled with loud shrieks except for a single lecherous old prostitute, who tried every possible means to get it into her, but without success.

Having become notorious for his extraordinary endowment, Aocao found no woman willing to marry him. Alone at home, he could not but feel lonely and bereft.

By that time Empress Wu was already over sixty.

Princess Qianjin introduced to her a man called Feng Xiaoyao,[45] to whom the Empress showed great favor. Xiaoyao had been a rascal selling potions in the city of Chang'an before entering the palace. He had an endowment both large and hard, and with some medicinal aphrodisiacs applied to it, was capable of tireless intercourse with women for a whole night. The empress fell deeply in love with him. On the pretext that she needed a man with clever ideas, she had him tonsured as a monk, gave him the religious name, Xue Huaiyi,[46] and thereafter often summoned him into the palace to supervise work, which provided her with excellent opportunities to tryst with him. Huaiyi was therefore promoted to the chief stewardship and enfeoffed with a dukedom.

When he became rich and powerful, Huaiyi became haughty and arrogant. He not only kept a large harem outside [the palace], but also started to contend with the court-physician Shen Huaiqiu[47] for the empress' favor. In a fit of fury, his jealousy erupted and he set fire to the Yanming Hall of the

45 Princess Qianjin, the eighteenth daughter of Emperor Gaozu, was about the same age as Gaozong.

46 The reason Empress Wu changed his surname to Xue was because her daughter Princess Taiping's husband was surnamed Xue, and the Empress was therefore able to tell people that Xue Huaiyi was an uncle of her son-in-law.

47 In the official histories, his name is given as Shen Nanqiu.

White Horse Temple,[48] [and as a result] Empress Wu consulted with [her daughter] Princess Taiping, and then had some strong palace- women tie him up and kill him.[49] When his corpse was carried back to the temple, he was reported to have died of a sudden illness.

Shen Huaiqiu, who was skilled in the arts of the bedchamber, and hence was also promoted , was not, in the end, equal the empress in sexual stamina, and collapsed after lengthy service to her. He died of seminal depletion.

Empress Wu had now turned seventy.

Although she was of advanced age, she maintained her health so well that her teeth showed no sign of deterioration,[50] her hair remained as thick and smooth as before, and her body was ripe with the seductive allure of a young woman. With her vital powers well- conserved, she developed an ever-stronger desire for carnal indulgence. No one, whether a veteran prostitute or a lascivious wench, was able to equal her in lewdness.

It so happened that at that time someone introduced to her Zhang Changzong,[51] a beautiful youth with an enormous penis. In her interview with him Empress Wu found him indeed supremely handsome and attractive.

Changzong then introduced to her his elder brother Yizhi,[52] who was also fair-complexioned and had an oversized male organ. After having tried him out, the empress concluded that he also lived up to her expectations.

Both brothers then became her favorite lovers. They were respectively appointed Director of Horses and Carriages[53] and Director of the Library and the Archives,[54] and were granted fiefdoms as well.[55] There was not a single

---

48 In fact, Xue Hauiyi set fire to the Ming Tang (Hall of Light), part of the palace compound, not to the Yanming Hall of the White Horse Temple. The Hall of Light, described in detail in many sources, was the most magnificent building in the capital, and its destruction was an act of massive vandalism.

49 According to *Zizhi tongjian* (Comprehesive Mirror for Aid in Government), Xue Huaiyi was killed by Prince of Jianchang, Wu Youning, and his stalwart bodyguards. See *Zizhi tongjian*, vol. 14, p. 6502. Other sources, including the official Tang History, credit Princess Taiping and her palace attendants.

50 In fact, when the empress was sixty-nine years old, she grew a new tooth and she took this as a sign of her longevity and therefore changed the reign- name to Changshou, meaning "longevity."

51 The Zhang brothers' grand uncle, Zhang Xingcheng, served in the early years of Gaozong's reign as Prime Minister.

52 Because of source contradictions, it is not clear whether Yizhi and Changzong were brothers or cousins. Most commentators believe them to be brothers.

53 Director of Horses and Carriage was an official rank of 3b in the Tang dynasty. See *Xin Tangshu*, vol. 4, p. 1253.

54 Director of the Library and the Archives was an official of rank 3b in Tang dynasty. See *Xin Tangshu*, vol. 4, p. 1214.

person, either inside or outside the palace, who did not stand in awe of them. All and sundry called Changzong, "Chancellor Six" and Yizhi "Chancellor Five," and likened the beautiful Chancellor Six to a lotus flower.

In the second year of the Tianshou period (691) when winter set in, Empress Wu, seized by a whim to enjoy the bloom of flowers, decided to make an excursion with Changzong and Yizhi to Shangyuan, the imperial park.[56] She issued an edict to her officials:

To Shangyuan I'll go tomorrow,
Posthaste you should let spring know.
Overnight must flowers grow,
Make sure no morning wind will blow.[57]

Obeying her edict, hundreds of flowers were in blossom the next morning, and because of this, people nowadays still call the tenth month[58] *xiao yangchun* (small spring). Does this mean that Heaven, too, succumbed to the will of the Empress? A contemporary scholar wrote a quatrain in commemoration of this unusual phenomenon, and focused his attention on the flower-like beauty of Changzong:

After the audience the Empress went out into sunlight,
An edict urgent brought an early spring to her sight.
Everywhere were flowers with various colors of mix,
Yet the most beautiful was Lotus, the Chancellor Six.

There was another poem, written by a contemporary of the time, describing how Changzong resembled a reincarnation of Wang Zijin[59] as he,

---

55 Changzong was granted the Dukedom of Ye, and Yizhi, the Dukedom of Heng, each governing three hundred households. The titles were honorary, but the revenues were substantial.

56 Shangyuan, also called Shanglinyuan, was built in the Latter Han, and its location was in the eastern quarter of the city of Luoyang.

57 According to *Tangshi jishi* (Historical Events explaining Tang Poetry), Empress Wu, in the third year of the Tianshou reign-period (692), actually issued such an edict, written in poetic form. Both official histories of the Tang mention the edict.

58 The tenth month in the Chinese lunar calendar is roughly equal to December on the Western calendar.

59 Wang Zijin, or Wang Ziqiao, is a character in Chinese mythology. It is said that after thirty years of Daoist meditation on Mount Song, he became a Daoist immortal and ascended to Heaven riding a crane. The Chinese crane has a spot of bright scarlet on its head, the color representing pure *yang* essence which symbolizes vitality and life. The empress, in her last years, created a new government body called the Institute of the Crane, which, presided over by the Zhang brothers and staffed by handsome young men, soon acquired the reputation of a male harem.

by order of the Empress, rode on a colorfully-painted wooden crane with a robe of feathers draped about him:

In talent you could equal Fuqiu Bao of olden times,[60]
And were as beautiful as Ding Lingwei[61] *in appearance.*
Had historiography not linked your name with crimes,
Oh, Zhonglang,[62] *who could deny your unparalleled eminence?*

Changzong and Yizhi took turns to enter the palace every other night to serve the empress. On the days they were off duty, they would seek the company of beautiful women, indulging themselves in wine and orgiastic revelry all through the night. No wonder they were often tired as they lay down with their empress, and without sufficient energy would from time to time fail to maintain their erection. Empress Wu, of course, was not satisfied.

This was the second year of Yanzai (694).[63]

One day, after a banquet, the empress sat in the Happy Spring Garden enjoying the enchanting scene and the balmy air. Flowers were falling, piling layer upon layer on the ground; catkins were flying, lighting on her clothes. Hidden birds were chirping merrily with neither the male nor the female willing to be outshone by the others' high notes. Bees and butterflies darted up and down busying themselves in a search for right spot on each flower to mount their invasions. Deeply moved by these sights and sounds, the empress felt amorous, and was filled with a desire to disport herself immediately in the bedchamber with Changzong and his brother. Still, she hesitated to summon them, thinking that they might be too exhausted to meet her demands. She sighed.

Noticing her restlessness, the eunuch Niu Jinqing[64] climbed the flight of stairs and asked, "Is something troubling Your Majesty today? Are you missing your favorite son, the Prince of Luling, so long absent?"[65]

Jinqing actually knew very well what the Empress was sighing for. His inquiry had a purpose.

---

60 Fuqiu Bao was an erudite scholar in the Han dynasty. It is said that he was a student of the more-famous Xun Qing (313–238 B.C.E.).

61 A character in Chinese mythology, reputed to be extremely handsome..

62 *Zhonglang* refers to Zhang Changzong. It was one of the official titles granted him by the empress.

63 There was only one year in *Yanzai* period. In the following year (695), the reign-name was changed to "*Zhengsheng*." The author purposely makes a mistake about the year here. Cf. note 76.

64 Niu Jinqing is a fictitious character. In history there was an official named Zong Jinqing, but he was not a eunuch.

65 The Prince of Luling was her son, Zhongzong, whom she had deposed and exiled.

The empress was vexed.

"How stupid you are to ask a question like this!" she said. "You, old servant, have been working a long time in the palace. How can you still not know me?"

Jinqing prostrated himself on the ground at once and then ventured to say, "At the risk of beheading, I, your humble servant, wish to say something important to Your Majesty."

"Go ahead!" said the empress. "I will not punish you."

Jinqing continued:

"Observing your holy condition, I have found that men like Yizhi and Changzong are often not good enough to sate Your Majesty's desire."

"Ah, you are right, smart boy!" said the empress, breaking into a grin.

"In my view," Jinqing went on, "Yizhi and Changzong have abused their wealth and power. They derided you as being senile and were often unwilling to fulfill their duties if not summoned again and again. Their attendance was forced and their affection was unnatural. They pretended they enjoy your charms, but in fact they did not. That was why they were feeble in merrymaking and [their erections] shrink even before Your Majesty has achieved total gratification. And, Gracious Lady, it is rumored that their mansions have been filled with singing boys and dancing girls on top of the bevies of beautiful concubines they possess. How can they serve Your Majesty heart and soul?"

The empress fumed.

"I have been deceived by these slaves!" she cursed. "They claimed that their energy was exhausted and it never dawned on me that they had other women. I can rid myself of them like meat on my table!"

"Pray calm your fury, Gracious Lady," said Jinqing. "They are not worth smearing your sharpening stone. I have someone, a handsome young man about thirty years of age, to introduce to you. This young man lives in the city of Luoyang, and his name is Xue Aocao. He is endowed not only with beauty and talent, but with a virile member much larger than those of Yizhi and Changzong. Your Majesty needs simply to issue an order to authorize me to bring him to the palace. Surely he will be able to serve Your Majesty well, and his company, whenever needed, shall be guaranteed."

"Do you know him?" asked the empress.

"No, I do not know him personally," Jinqing replied. "But according to what the young men in his neighborhood have said, his endowment is so large that they cannot even wrap their hands around it nor measure it by a ruler. Its head is similar to a snail, its body resembles a skinned rabbit, and its veins look like worms. They also claimed that it could bear the weight of a bag of grain without bending even slightly."

Empress Wu, her back reclining against a screen, heaved a sigh.

"Pray say no more," she said. "I have understood."

She ordered a servant to take out from the Imperial Treasury two gold ingots, two pieces of white jade in a round, flat shape, four bolts of colorful brocade, and a carriage with four horses,[66] and personally drew up a summons, which ran:

> *Occupied with myriad of state affairs, I have long lacked a private moment to heed my own secret yearnings: to invite a man of supreme talent for an intimate chat. I have heard that your aspirations are lofty, just as your endowment is great and indeed extraordinary, and I am anxious to make your acquaintance to allay my longings. Detailed instructions regarding requirements and specifications will be given you upon your arrival, and it is my sincere wish that you not be so proud and aloof as to refuse my kindness.*

Carrying the edict as well as the gold and the brocade, Jinqing went to call upon Aocao, who, on seeing the envoy, said, "I am of humble origin and might profane the august virtue of Her Majesty. I am not a worthy person and must beg your pardon for my inability to obey your order."

"Sir," said Jinqing, "if you miss this golden opportunity for a rapid advance in your career, you might all your life remain a common fellow languishing in your neighborhood."

"There are proper ways to advance," said Aocao. "It is shameful to use one's sexual organ for social climbing!"

"Do you think that you can fly so far and high as to leave this world?" the eunuch whispered in his ear. "Besides, you have only scarce knowledge of intercourse. Who else would be able to accommodate you except Her Majesty?"

Aocao saw no option but to accompany him.

On the road he sighed, "A man of ability should advance through his talent. What subject is there in the Civil Service Examinations that is designed for what has today recommended me?"

Jinqing sped away and reported to the empress, who dispatched at once both officials and guards on horseback to welcome her guest. On his arrival, Aocao was ushered by Jingqing into the presence of the empress in the Rear Hall. He kowtowed, and then at her order, took a seat and was served tea. When he was finished with his tea, the empress ordered her female attendants to conduct him to the Translucent Jade Bedchamber to be bathed.

---

66 Only a high official was entitled to ride in a carriage drawn by four horses.

The bath that the empress ordered for him was called the "marrow-refreshing spa bath." All the female attendants waiting upon him removed their clothing, and tempted by their alluring sensuality, his penis naturally stiffened, rising huge and riotous under their watchful eye. They could not help but giggle and had to cover their mouths with their hands.

"Her Majesty has found the right person!" they whispered.

After having bathed, Aocao was given a fresh set of apparel–a coat resembling a hovering crane in the clouds, a sword inlaid with seven precious objects[67] accompanied by a belt, and an emerald cap of majestic splendor which bore on its top a black kerchief. He put them on, looking from a distance as beautiful as a celestial being.

The empress was delighted. Clapping her hands, she exclaimed, "An immortal has descended into my residence!"

At her bidding, a meal was immediately served. Jinqing was invited and the three of them sat around the table eating and drinking. The drinking vessels they used were ruby goblets in the shape of a lotus flower,[68] and the beverage was a renowned grape wine made in Xiliang.[69] They drank several toasts, and Aocao was about to quaff another when he noticed that the empress, her face slightly reddened, was quite aroused. With her interest no longer in wine, she instructed those waiting on her to go prepare the East Chamber of the Huaqing Palace with soft and warm bedclothes, and after telling Jinqing to depart, she repaired there with Aocao, hand in hand.

Inside the chamber they sat side by side. Two young maids entered holding a golden basin of water bestrewn with rose petals. No sooner had they placed the basin in the room than the empress waved them off. She closed the golden-phoenix door herself and latched it with the nine-dragon bolt. However, the female attendants working outside could still peep through the door chinks to see what was happening inside as they were passing by, and consequently learned each and every detail of the ensuing scene.

Empress Wu was now washing her intimate parts in the rose water.

She asked Aocao, "Jinqing told me that you are still a virgin and have yet to experience nuptial delight. Is that true?"

---

[67] There are, in the Buddhist scriptures, a variety of explanations about the seven precious objects. According to *Lotus Sutra*, they refer to: 1) gold, 2) silver, 3) colored glaze, 4) tridacna, 5 agate, 6) pearl, 7) rose.

[68] The emperors of the Tang dynasty, claiming that they were offspring of the Daoist philosopher Lao Tzu (his real name was Li Dan), worshipped Daoism. But Empress Wu, since she had joined the Buddhist order before re-entering the palace, more interested in Buddhism than Daoism. The lotus flower is the symbol of Buddhism.

[69] Xiliang is located in the western part of present-day Gansu province.

"It is a very unfortunate matter that my endowment is oversized," he replied, "and for this very reason, I have for many, many years remained unwed. Today an imperial command has brought me here, and I do not know, in my state of trepidation, what to show to Your Majesty. Since my contour is wretched and my fleshly form unrefined, I am afraid that I might not be sufficiently qualified for the services I am to perform to Your Majesty's holy configuration. Pray allow your female attendants to have a look at my nether region first. It is my humble suggestion that Your Majesty proceed no further till you have received their favorable review. A sudden exposure of my frame to your Majesty's eyes might too strongly stir your senses, and I fear I might not be able to make amends even though I died ten thousand deaths."

"Your object is really so large?" asked the empress. "I would fain see it."

She bade Aocao remove his underclothes, and remaining seated, looked askance at his organ, which indeed appeared huge, both in length and girth. For long moments, she could not take her eyes off it.

"Sir," she then said jokingly, "you must depart at once, for I cannot tolerate so extraordinarily fearsome a man as you!"

In the meanwhile she reached out her hand to fondle his still-limp sexual organ. "How large this beastly thing is!" she remarked. "And it has not yet experienced sexual congress!"

She unbuttoned her garb, openly displaying her nether regions, the pubic area a little engorged, and the surrounding flesh plump and hairless. Aocao did not dare to touch her. The empress seized his hand and guided it to her private parts. He followed her directions as he stroked her, and his penis gradually rose. Suddenly it straightened fully, and the concavities around the club-like head all filled up, with the veins and ridges protruding visibly. She seized it the moment she saw it standing stiff, as if she had obtained a most valuable treasure.

"What an enormous treasure!" she exclaimed. "It is, to be sure, not an earthly thing. I have seen many men and yet not single one of them possessed an object like this. In ancient times there was Wang Yifu[70] whose "livid handle"[71] was as smooth and bright as white jade, and the member of no other man could match it for beauty. Since your member too, is of surpassing beauty, I should name it 'white jade livid handle'."

She fondled it tenderly.

---

70 An historical personage living in the Six Dynasties. The reference to his unusual endowment is lost.

71 "Livid handle" (*zhubing*) is, of course, a euphemism for penis; and while the unusual term probably connotes something pale, colorless or ashen, we use "livid" which has the additional connotation in English, of "angry."

In a state of sweet confusion she was overwhelmed with lustful sensations and threw herself onto her back, with her head resting on the "pillow of immortality" made in Qiuci,[72] and her hips bolstered up with a cushion in the shape of a crescent-moon. Lifting her legs high, he positioned himself between them, while she guided him into herself with both her hands. At the beginning, the empress' vagina was rather dry and he found it hard to cleave a smooth entrance into her.

"Go slowly," said the empress.

Impelled to enter swiftly, Aocao battered her with his lusty thrusts. The empress, uncomfortable in accepting him, frowned with her eyebrows and clenched her teeth, still only managing to sheath the tip of his instrument. It was not until a stream of fluid had lubricated her, and her conduit had become smooth, that he was able to wedge himself further in. Still suffering as he drove even deeper, the empress quickly reached into her bedside drawer and withdrew a piece of twine which she tied around his organ to mark the midpoint.

"Both the size and the stiffness of your "livid handle" are beyond my ability to endure with comfort," she said. "It hurts me so much that I cannot stand the pain. You must cease for a few moments. But then start again."

Before long, Aocao felt her squirm her body toward him, her eyes dull, her hands burning, and her cheeks turning vermilion. She gasped, and as her female fluids rose up, he swiftly resumed his penetration and began to thrust in and out, enduring for two hundred strokes. In an ecstatic trance, the empress clasped his waist and moaned, her voice thrilled, her eyes closed, her sweet perspiration covering her body, and her limbs splayed out on the cushion, languorous.

"Royal Majesty," he asked, "are you all right?"

The empress made no response.

He was about to withdraw when she quickly embraced him, saying, "Oh my darling son, leave it inside me until I am completely satisfied."

Once again Aocao thrust into her, each time driving in vigorously, yet withdrawing gently. After about a hundred more strokes, the empress' fluids were secreting in abundance, and soaked the piece of twine she had tied around his "livid handle."

"Oh, my love! How well you satisfy me!" she blurted, caressing his shoulders tenderly. "I should grant you the title: Lord of Perfect Satisfaction.

---

72 Qiuci is in present-day Xinjiang Autonomous Region.

Next year I am going to change the reign-title, and I shall call it the Reign of Perfect Satisfaction (*ruyi*)!"[73]

"Royal Majesty, it is amazing how full you are with vigor and vitality," Aocao flattered her. "Your features and complexion are so well-preserved, and blossom with good health! You seem to me little more than a youthful maiden, so radiant is your pristine glow! As your humble servant, I would consider it my greatest honor to be able to provide you with the satisfaction you desire. In my previous years of living in this mortal world, I have never been able to embrace even one single woman. The pleasure Your Majesty has given to me is thus more exquisite than any I have ever known. For my part, I have been more than fulfilled, yet Your Majesty must have suffered greatly as my ugly object took liberties with your jade body. Oh, how numerous are the offences I have committed upon you! I cannot count them even on the hairs of my head! I wish only that Your Majesty not forsake me. I would die content should I be permitted to continue serving you in this very bedchamber."

"Lord of Perfect Satisfaction," she said, "even if you did not slacken your services to me, I would never for a single moment forget you. From now on, do not call yourself 'servant' nor address me as 'Majesty'. You and I are as intimate as husband and wife and all the protocols between sovereign and subject should therefore apply to us no more."

"Since I have brought upon myself no unforeseen disaster," said Aocao, "I can but consider myself the most fortunate person in the world. How could I dare expect Your Majesty to condescend to me so kindly? Your loving affection toward me is already so very profound!"

Now busily engaged in talking and joking, he was unaware that his "livid handle," though still lodged inside her, had slightly slowed in its motion.

"Are you tired?" she asked.

"Not yet," he answered. "I haven't had nearly enough!"

"You are just beginning to learn how to employ that object and you don't know quite yet how to enjoy its pleasures," said the empress. "It takes time to taste its greatest delights. You must not stop if I have yet to be satisfied."

Aocao raised her legs again.

"Wait a moment," he said, and hastily fetching a towel, smoothed it over her nether parts and then wiped his own organ dry. After stimulating himself to another erection, he re-entered her.

---

73 The empress did, in fact, proclaim a reign-title of "perfect satisfaction." The term "*ruyi*," however, has a specialized meaning in Buddhist terminology, and refers to the Buddha-of-the- future. In view of the empress' well-known fondness for Buddhism, most scholars have tended to see this as the inspiration for the new reign-title.

"What a hungry man you are!" she said. "I might never be able to satisfy your insatiable appetite."

She then wished to rest for a short time, but at the sight of Aocao aflame with lust, re-positioned herself in a posture to receive him. The more he thrust, the more delighted she became. Recklessly, she rocked and squirmed, her fluids gushing, and her jasper gate, filled with steaming heat, bubbled with incessant gurgling sounds. Aocao lifted his body and then pounded into her harder than ever.

The empress embraced him tightly. "Oh my dear Lord of Perfect Satisfaction! How cruel you are!" she moaned in an affected tone. "I almost died, expiring at the climax of my pleasure!"

For a long while they remained entwined in each other's arms.

"Let us stop now," she said. "We must not overindulge ourselves."

"Then what was the purpose of this invitation?" said Aocao. "If Your Majesty wishes to treat me with kindness, you should not fear my oversized belly."

"Sir, how much do you eat and drink?" she asked.

"I eat as if to fill a huge gully and drink as if to drown a river," he replied.

"Well, well," said the empress, "if what you said is true, Lord of Perfect Satisfaction, you are bound to consume a huge amount of your hostess."

"Needless to say, Madam," he replied. "But I dearly wish that Your Majesty could accommodate me, for I am now beside myself, burning up with the flame of passion!"

He stealthily loosened two turnings of the twine and penetrated her more deeply.

Feeling a sudden twinge in the very center of her delight, the empress knew that he must have done something without her knowledge.

"Dare you take liberties without permission?" she burst out.

"Royal Madam, my audacity is but a little test of your generosity to me,"[74] he said. "Should you be able to tolerate me further, I would very much appreciate it."

"Toleration is certainly a fine virtue," said the empress. "But what if one person revels in pleasure while the other suffers pain?"

Aocao took no notice of her words and forced the entry of another two inches. The empress, being unable to bring herself to part with him, had no alternative but to yield to his assault. He thrust inward this way and that until

---

74 This sentence, *guanguo si zhi ren yi* in the original, is a quotation from Confucius's *Lun Yu* (The Analects), and D. C. Lau has translated it as follows: "Observe the errors and you will know the man." See *The Analects*, trans. D. .C. Lau, chapter IV, p. 73.

he felt he was about to ejaculate. As a man inexperienced in sex, he had not the vaguest idea that his penetration had reached the deepest niche of the empress' orifice.

The niche of a woman, located in the innermost recess, is fleshy, and resembles in shape the slightly-opened bud of a flower. When a man's glans touches it, he can feel its contracting pressure and will then feel a delight throughout his entire body, a pleasure so great that it cannot be described. Conscious of the fiery tip piercing her innermost spot, the empress squeezed it hastily and kept it in deep until he spent, his ejaculation filling her with an enormous rapture. Having long been living in celibacy, Aocao shot his sperm like a waterspout, which joined with her female fluids to form a surging torrent gushing forth.

The empress clutched him tightly.

After a while she said, "I am worn out."

She wiped her privates with her undergarments, got up, and ordered the door to be opened. Looking out she found that it was already late afternoon.

She then had a feast laid out in the front veranda and dined with Aocao. Her happiness being at its height, she summoned Niu Jinqing and promoted him to the position of the Lieutenant of Imperial Entrance Guards.[75] She also conferred upon him the title of Supervisor of the Inner Services and granted him a golden casket containing a full measure of pearls, two silver caskets filled with gold, silks of different colors, and thirty-thousand strings of cash.

"You are superior to Wei Wuzhi!"[76] exclaimed the empress, after rewarding him. "Not even with thousands of pieces of gold and jade could I sufficiently repay you."

The next day Empress Wu proclaimed the inauguration of the reign-title "Perfect Satisfaction"[77] and also granted an amnesty in which the pardons and remissions of punishments exceeded what had normally been permitted.

The Prime Minister, Yang Zhirou,[78] raised an objection.

"After receiving the edict of Your Majesty," he said, "officials have been rather confused about the meaning of the new reign title. It seems neither a symbol of good fortune nor is it related to the principles or the achievements of your administration. I suggest you use another name."

"It is I who ordered the name to be thus changed," the empress shouted. "Who dares to disagree with me?"

---

75 Lieutenant of Imperial Entrance Guards was an official of rank 3b in the Tang.

76 Wei Wuzhi introduced Chen Ping (?–178 B.C.E.) to Liu Bang, for whom Chen Ping designed six ingenious strategies which helped Liu establish the Han dynasty.

77 Historically, the reign period of Perfect Satisfaction was 692.

78 The official Tang histories suggest that Yang was a sycophant of the empress.

She removed Yang from his position.

Everyone else at the court was flabbergasted and all of them ceased their babbling on this subject.

The empress was now so deeply in love with Aocao, that she resolved to deprive the Zhang brothers of their official positions and properties, and award them to him. She also considered building a mansion for him.

He declined her offer.

"Your Majesty has a large number of favorites," he said, "and this is no doubt very harmful to your reputation as a sovereign of virtue. For this reason, I beg Your Majesty not to grant me anything. Besides, you know I am single; a big mansion is entirely useless to me."

The empress could do no more than defer to his wishes.

The next year, the consorts Liu and Wu of the Emperor Expectant[79] happened to learn, after some prying, the real meaning of "Perfect Satisfaction." They remarked, "Aocao's member is as large as that a mule, and yet Empress Wu can receive it without the slightest discomfort!"

On hearing their gossip, the empress flew into a towering rage. "Those bitches dared to laugh at me!" she cursed, and then ordered both women to commit suicide.

The empress was by nature suspicious. When Gaozong had been alive, numerous concubines and female attendants had been executed by her under a variety of pretexts simply because she had been suspicious of them. Now due to Aocao's intervention, a great number of palace women escaped her punishment.

Having now developed an extreme intimacy with Aocao, Empress Wu would habitually place her legs across his thighs as they sat together, or entwine herself in his arms while sleeping. They enjoyed tremendously their carnal affinity.

One day the empress expressed to him her most profound and loving affection.

"Reading *The Annals of Spring and Autumn*,"[80] she said, "I was surprised at the Duke of Jin's infatuation with his concubine Liji. I thought he must have been crazy to kill his heir apparent, Shensheng, and banish his own sons Yiwu and Chang'er without feeling guilty. Now that I have deeply fallen in love with

---

79 Historically, Empress Wu had the consorts Liu and Dou (not Wu) executed. See *Xin Tangshu*, vol. 11, p. 3489.

80 This is the earliest annalistic history of China, believed to have been written by Confucius, and hence numbered among the Five Classics .

you, I can't help but laugh at the Duke of Jin as I compare myself with him, for his love of Liji seems to me now rather superficial."

Aocao was astonished.

"When I first entered the palace," he said, "the exile of the Heir Apparent to Luling had been completed. Obviously it is not appropriate to compare me with that concubine since I did nothing to sow discord between you and your son. Outsiders, should they hear Your Majesty's words, might wrongly blame me, which is bound to cause me a great deal of difficulty."

The empress comforted him. "It is simply because I have so doted on you," she said, "that I unwittingly made such an indiscreet remark."

In the second month of the first year of Yanzai (694),[81] the empress had a pleasant pavilion built in the inner garden and invited Aocao to drink with her. When she was in the middle stages of intoxication she laughed and babbled lustfully to him, "You have had intercourse with me many times, but never once did you put the whole length of your livid handle into me."

At her bidding, a gilded, exquisitely-decorated tent was set up in the pavilion. The Empress took him into her arms, saying, "Let us indulge ourselves without restraint today. You may insert the entire length into me, but take care to do so with caution."

"Royal Madam, there is in fact not much of it that has been left unused," said Aocao. "You know I did my utmost in my services to make Your Majesty royally satisfied. Today Your Majesty is in such high spirits that you are willing to permit me a deeper penetration, but what if you end up in pain? Then all my loyal efforts would be wasted."

"Do not worry," she said. "I fear only that you might thrust too hard and too fast. If you go gently, there is certainly nothing to fear."

She laid her head on a high pillow and bolstered her waist with a folded quilt. Aocao, holding his "livid handle," placed it against her vulva. Instead of entering immediately into the opening, however, he moved only in mild gyrations to moisten the tip of his organ.

Trembling with eager desire, how the Empress wished that he would thrust straight into her deepest recesses without delay!

Aocao, however, purposely postponed his full insertion, and made only shallow motions at the gate of her grotto until a stream of coital juices flowed, like excretions from an escargot. The empress was about to compel his compliance when Aocao abruptly withdrew.

"You scurvy knave," cooed the empress in honeyed tones. "Why did you withdraw?"

---

[81] Notice the author's confusion of time here. Cf. note 62.

Obligingly, he immediately re-entered her. Pausing at the point where she had once tied her twine, he asked, "Is Your Majesty feeling all right with so deep a penetration?"

She smiled, her eyes remaining closed.

"Don't quicken your stroke," she said.

Turning a deaf ear to what she said, Aocao inserted another two or three inches.

"Too much!" she screeched.

He then bent down a little, and raised her buttocks with his hands to see how well she was taking him. As he noticed that with his gentle motions she was becoming highly excited, he inserted another two or three inches.

"How wonderful!" she exclaimed. "I have now reached a state I have never before experienced. I am dying!"

Though rather limp in her delirium of pleasure, the empress, her tone trembling, and her breathing broken, lifted her legs and set her feet across his shoulders. Then, with all her might rolled her hips ten times or so, while he seized her hips and rocked back and forth with her in a quick tempo.

"Are you hot and itchy down there?" he asked, teasingly.

"No words can describe how good I am feeling," the empress answered. "I am wondering how much of it has yet to enter?"

"About two inches," he said.

"It feels as if it is getting larger inside me," she said. "You had better slow down to ensure that you won't drive all the way to the hilt."

"But in my state of ecstasy," he panted, "I am no longer able to contain myself."

Aocao rammed forcefully into her until he had gained complete admission, leaving virtually no room for a single hair to squeeze in. The empress was beside herself with rapture. Voluptuously she snuggled close to him, rocking and wriggling as vehemently as she could. After a hundred times or so she came to a halt and looking at him, said weakly, "Darling, let's take a break now. I am feeling very dizzy and don't know what is going to happen to me."

At the height of his ardor, Aocao continued without surcease. Pleasure had overtaken him and he had been carried away. After another hundred thrusts or so, wisps of heat emitted from her vagina.

"Oh my sweet daddy, I am dying!" she cried. "Cease! I really cannot endure any more!"

Aocao paid no attention, and went on pumping and pounding as before. The female essences of the empress were exuding and dripping, making sounds like those one might hear when several men are wading through a puddle. Presently, her limbs were stretched out and she was swooning, her eyes shut, teeth clenched, and her breathing becoming weaker and weaker. He was alarmed at the sight of her coma and hastily pulled himself out and helped her sit up. It took her a long while to come around.

"My dear Royal Madam, what is the matter?" he asked upon her revival. "I was terrified by what has happened to you and dare not do it with you again."

The empress stared at him for some moments before embracing him.

"Never ever again be so rash!" she said, with tears in her eyes. "If you had not desisted and I had passed away, how would you have handled the situation?"

"Royal Madam," he murmured, "I was not aware that I could make you lose consciousness. How terrifying it was! I am impotent now, unable to engage further with you."

Because of his shock, Aocao's "livid handle" had shrunk.

"We'd better stop now," said the empress. "How fortunate for you that I didn't die and that you can later on, continue to enjoy my body!"

She laid her head upon his lap, and in a lascivious manner, teased his genitals with her cheeks.

"I have always been preoccupied with yearnings for a man of extraordinary ability," she said. "But never had I expected that Jinqing would find me a fellow with so huge a member. My regret is constant that I did not encounter you earlier. Now that I have been blessed to possess you, I hope only that you won't be "in like a lion and out like a lamb," like Yizhi and his brother."

"Surely I won't!" said Aocao. "Should I dare to be unfaithful to Your Majesty, may God punish me! Royal Madam, you hold the power over my life. Should you find me in any way failing to keep my word, execute me with your sword and tear my body into a thousand pieces! I would regret only that I would not know what would become of Your Majesty afterwards. I had been an utterly useless person before making your acquaintance. Had it not been for meeting Your Majesty, the taste of so delicious a pleasure beneath the skirt would have been unimaginable to me!"

"No one but I can receive you," she said, "and no one but you is able to satisfy me. I still remember my experience while serving Taizong[82] at the age of fourteen. Though his member was only of medium size, it hurt me so much that I could not bear it, since I was at the time very young. Consequently, during the entire first six months of sleeping with him, I experienced no pleasure at all. When I was twenty-six or twenty-seven years old, I began to serve Gaozong and he was much larger and harder, so far as that part of him

82 See note 6.

was concerned. But every time he had sex with me, he cared only about his own enjoyment and rarely was he so considerate as to start or stop out of consideration for my gratification. Fortunately, after his death I met Huaiyi, the monk, whose endowment, though appearing at the beginning not so large as that of Gaozong, would gradually grow longer, harder, and hotter once it had entered my furnace, and his engagement with me could last a whole night without stopping for a wink of sleep. Also very virile was Shen Huaiqiu, my late personal physician. In order to satisfy me, he never rested, even after ejaculating. His overexertion eventually made him ill and brought about his death. The two brothers Changzong and Yizhi, who had been with me from time to time before you, are both beautiful youths. While Yishi was remarkable for the great size of his organ, Changzong's was more typical in length, which was about six or seven inches. Both of them could provide me with much pleasure. The only problem was that after ejaculating, they could not achieve another erection, and sometimes, even in the midst of our activity, they became impotent. How I resented them because of this! All those men I have just now told you about are among the most outstanding in the world. Nevertheless, in comparison with my Lord of Perfect Satisfaction, they are hardly worth mentioning. From now on, Sir Might, you need not thrust all the way to the root. Enter half of your object, and for me, it should be enough!"

The empress was at the time in her twilight years.

Still, however, she retained her beauty and sexual allure. Her teeth and hair, kept in excellent condition, remained little changed. However, with such a large gap in their ages, one being young and the other approaching the last phase of life, it was inevitable that their coition would harm one while benefiting the other.

This was why Aocao often looked exhausted.

One day he and the empress reposed in the Jinfang Palace. Crab-apple trees outside the front veranda were in full bloom, and the empress plucked a flower to decorate her hair. As she reclined against a green screen, she enticingly bared half of her buxom breasts, and seductively ogled Aocao, gazing at him from the corner of her eye. Instantly, he was set aflame. He moved to her side and pressed his mouth against hers. And no sooner had blankets been spread on the floor, than he leapt upon her, their sport lasting until both had achieved total satisfaction.

Later, and needless to say, they made love in the same fashion many times.

On one of those occasions, their copulation completed, the empress left to preside over her morning court. Changzong and Yizhi were among the officials present, yet she did not so much as cast a glance their way, much less offer them any gifts. Nor did she summon them to a private meeting after the court session was over. The two brothers were surprised at her change of attitude. In spite of their suspicions, however, they knew nothing of the cause.

One day, on a visit to the Hualin Garden, the empress summoned all the scholars of the Northern Gate, including Changzong and Yizhi, and entertained them with an extravagant banquet. Changzong's cheeks looked as beautiful as a peach blossom and his smile was alluring, full of charm. The empress was aroused at the sight of his bewitching appearance and ordered each of the brothers to toast her longevity with a jade goblet. Raising his glass, Changzong deliberately revealed a portion of his arm, which appeared almost the same color of jade. Unable to restrain herself, the empress pinched his tender muscle with her nails and told Changzong, as the feast was drawing to a close, to return to the palace with her. This invitation naturally led him to the expectation of making love with her. However, as they reached the gate of the palace, the empress stopped.

"I cannot do it with you," she said, gazing upon him with affection for some while. "But trust me. I love you as dearly as before."

She instructed her servants to give a thousand catties of gold to Changzong and another thousand ounces of gold to Yizhi. The receipt of such largess, to be sure, served only to deepen their suspicions. After making inquiries, the two brothers discovered that it was Aocao who enjoyed her favor, and they could do no more than sigh in vain.

The empress felt guilty. In order to show her kindness and affection, she paid visits to the Northern Gate[83] from time to time, and drank and flirted with the two brothers as if nothing had changed in their relationship. Often, she also bestowed gifts upon them.

But never again did she even once make use of their sexual services.

Now came the first year of the Yuantong period.[84]

Early in the summer when the skies had cleared after a shower, Empress Wu and Aocao took a stroll in the rear courtyard, hand in hand. Hearing the birds hidden in the thicket of green willows chirping and calling to each other, the empress was moved, and an impetuous desire abruptly surged into her mind.

"Even the birds know how to enjoy their conjugal relations," she sighed. "How can we humans be deprived of the same pleasures?"[85]

---

83 The Northern Gate in the Tang was where the Office of Academicians (Xueshi yuan) was located, and was where the academicians drafted decrees and wrote their views on the documents submitted to the emperor.

84 This is a fictitious reign-title. Judging from the context, it should be the historical *Shengli* reign-title, and the first year of *Shengli* was 698.

85 This sentence, with a little alteration, was later used by the Ming playwright Tang Xianzu

At her bidding, female attendants hastily fetched her embroidered blankets of Shu,[86] as well as her cushions and quilts, and spread them out at a secluded spot.

"Today, let us imitate the way birds make love!" she said, laughing.

They removed their lower garments. To perform the act of love in a different way, she lay prostrate on the blanket and then raised her buttocks into the air, telling Aocao to enter her from the rear. He did as she asked, and meanwhile reached out his hands to fondle her breasts, like a calf eager for milk from its mother. Their immeasurable delight, accompanied by intermittent pumping sounds, was indescribable.

One day the empress said to him, "The other day I saw Chancellor Six. Basking in the morning sunlight, there emanated from his body a lustrous beauty as wonderful as a lotus emerging from the water. Chancellor Five also appeared strikingly bright and charming."

"A gentleman is delighted to see other persons sharing their pleasure," he said. "Why not summon them, and let them serve Your Majesty at night?"

The empress laughed.

"Having had a taste of the fresh lichee from Nanhai,"[87] she said, "I cannot but feel that the plum is as insipid as wax. Nor do I find any further use for a small dollop of water, now that I have viewed the magnificence of the ocean. I would rather not summon them."

"But I am not jealous!" he said.

"Most certainly you are not a sour grape," the empress agreed. "It is just that I don't know how to deal with too much sweetness."

With this she burst out laughing.

The sixth month of that year was extremely hot. The empress found the only place that could provide her with some coolness was the Pavilion of Breezes, where she went to retire at night. A golden basin of water containing Longlin stones was placed in her sleeping chamber, sending out wafts of cold air, and her bedclothes, made of greenish gauze imported from a state called Quxu, were soft and dustproof, and a mat of split bamboo, imported from Korea, lay atop them. The empress would stretch out on the mat in a supine position, naked, while incense from Funan[88] burned at her bedside to repel mosquitoes.

(1550–1616) in his famous play *Mudan ting* (Peony Pavilion).

86 Present-day Sichuan province.

87 Nanhai ("southern sea") refers generically to the south of China.

88 Cambodia.

One night, as she slept soundly, Aocao crept in. Sidling up to her couch he found her nude body shining in the moonlight like a piece of jade, as beautiful as if it were a painting. He was stirred beyond endurance. He extracted his penis from his clothing and slowly inserted it into her vagina. The empress moaned in her dream. Presently she woke up, and opening her eyes, was astonished to find herself being mounted. By that time, she had already been the recipient of several thrusts.

"You dared to enter the forbidden chamber without my authorization!" she exclaimed joyfully. "What punishment do you suppose you should get?"

"Ay, my dear Royal Lady," Aocao teased back, "my entry into the Pink Gate[89] was a dangerous task, yet in facing such a risk I was thinking of no more than my loyalty to Your Majesty."

Amused by his repartee, the empress opened her thighs more widely to invite his ravishing assault. Instead of launching into a fierce attack, he raised her arms around his neck, lifted her two legs, and then, hefting her on himself, began to walk around in the room.

"My goodness," she cried out, giggling, "even the most lecherous prostitutes or the wildest women would shy away from trying this sort of lewd prank! Only you and I in this world can so wantonly indulge ourselves unrestrainedly in this sort of play!"

Later, on the night of mid-autumn, Aocao was invited to enjoy the moon at the Hall of Fairies in the Shangyang Palace. He drank toasts to the empress and conversed with her in an intimate undertone. Cheerful and lighthearted as he was on this happy occasion, he nevertheless could not help sighing, as peals of mirth brought him mixed feelings of joy and sadness. When happiness reaches its apogee, sadness is not far behind, and almost everyone has had this experience.

Among the palace women present, the most intelligent was Shangguan Wan'er, a consort of the second rank.[90] Always alert to the empress' intentions, she lifted her cup to drink a toast to her health and then began to sing:

Wind, the autumn wind, is blowing gently,

---

89 Hongmen, a place where Liu Bang, who later became the founding emperor of the Han dynasty, visited his rival Xiang Yu at great risk to his life and would have been killed but for the help of Fan Kuai and Zhang Liang, is, in Chinese, homophonous with "pink gate," a euphemism for vagina. Here Aocao is making a pun.

90 Shangguan Wan'er was Zhongzong's concubine. She also had an illicit relationship with Wu Sansi. Her grandfather Shangguan Yi was executed for treason against Empress Wu, and the empress, recognizing the girl's talent, brought her into the palace as a sort of private secretary to herself.

On the merry night of tranquility;
Dew, crystal dew, is shining brightly,
While the moon beams beautifully.
O, how I am honored to have the opportunity,
Of serving Your Heavenly Majesty;
As you and your celestial intimate immortal,
Enjoy each other affectionately.
Sir, why do you still appear so melancholy,
And sigh from time to time, so sadly?
Look, how numerous men of immortality,
Live on the moon, very lonely!

The Empress was delighted. She ordered Shangguan to sing a song to Aocao to urge him to imbibe more wine. Shangguan sang once again:

Bright, how very bright, is the moon tonight,
Breeze gentle and light brings aroma inside,
The palace at midnight is as joyful as in the daylight.
In the flight of love the phoenix-couple [91] delight,
Time is going by, and the younger days are finite,
May Sir Knight serve our Highness till she's satisfied.

Aocao drained his cup. Raising his re-filled vessel, he improvised a song to the empress;

The empyrean palace I could not see,
Its beautiful scene was concealed from me.
As far apart as soil and cloud we used to be,
How profoundly I am indebted to thee.
Long long live thine Imperial Majesty,
May thou like Heaven enjoy eternal longevity.
How I wish to follow thee to the heavenly city,
Soaring in the Milky Way with conviviality.

The song having been sung, Aocao, taking advantage of his intoxication, took the empress into his arms. No longer caring about the proprieties between sovereign and subject, he dipped one of her breasts in his goblet, drank half of the wine, and urged his empress to finish off the remaining half. She complied with pleasure.

Then, hand in hand, they went to retire to the Pavilion of Comfort. After a brief rest, the Empress removed her clothes, wearing nothing but her Lingnan petticoat. She encircled his neck with her arms, and ordered a female

91 Empress Wu and Xue Aocao.

attendant to fetch her a small fragrant Guilin cake. She chewed it slowly and then stuck out her tongue to share it with Aocao's mouth.

As she set one leg across him, he plunged his "livid handle" sideways into her vagina. Since both were highly aroused, the entrance was not difficult. Transported with delight, the empress turned her body further toward him, and this happy movement allowed her to engulf his entire length to the hilt. He kept it there and then agitated violently inside her. She felt no pain at all and called her female attendants to hold candles in their hands and stand nearer to her, and meanwhile bade Aocao to lie on his back. She sat astride him, and using her delicate hand guided his penis into her vagina. Now on top of him she bounced up and down until she had sheathed the largest part of his penis and only the scrotum, about three or four inches long, remained. He thrust upward into her.

"You knave!" she gasped, grinning. "You know you could make me die in your hands! Don't move! Let me watch how it enters and exits."

She bent to observe how they were joined, with her hands supporting herself on the couch. In overpowering orgasms, her profuse female fluids streamed out, and she had to change her towels five times. However, she showed no sign of fatigue until about the third watch of the night. By that time, she could hardly control her limbs with ease. Noticing that her weariness had reached the breaking point, Aocao let her lie down. He then mounted her and pounded her vigorously hundreds more times, each time driving all the way in to her deepest recesses. Her eyes closed, her loud moans and groans seemed endless.

"Oh, what pleasure!" she exclaimed. "This time is so very different, that I feel I am dying. Harder! Thrust into me harder! One more moment of such rapture and I will be happy to die without regrets!"

For a long while afterwards she said no more. Feeling that his discharge was imminent, he raised himself up and then thrust forward with all his strength. The empress clenched her teeth, and her face reddened.

"Oh my son," she blurted, "I really am dying!"

His sperm shot out like a spout of water.

Exhausted, finally, he drew himself out and lay down beside her. After having washed him with her towel, the empress laid her head on his thighs and let her face stroke his member. She then began to suck upon it and blushed red when she noticed that her female attendants, who were standing at the bedside with candles in their hands, had their curious eyes riveted on her oral activities.

"Come and lick it," she said to them. "Its head is so large that I suspect that you might not even be able to stretch your lips around it. But you can at least lick it to have a taste."

After a while she remarked, "Only I can deal with such a stupendous object, though on several occasions, I have almost failed to do so. Girls like yourselves, I believe, would probably have long been dead."

The female attendants only smirked, making no reply.

The Empress embraced Aocao tightly. When he was revived, she engaged him once again in copulation. He thrust in and out hundreds of times until she was limp, totally satiated.

One day she invited Aocao to drink with her when peonies in the rear courtyard were in blossom. They sat outdoors sipping their wine while viewing the blooming flowers.

"You are muscular and robust," said the tipsy empress. "Could you carry me in your arms and make love with me while strolling along in the garden?"

"Certainly," he replied.

They both removed their clothes, and he entered her after locking her arms around his neck and wrapping her two legs around his waist. They ambled around the flowery garden paths, and every few paces made a brief pause. A band of musicians was playing for them a tune called "The Red Peony Is Bright Before Me," with its words altered to accord with what was happening. The empress sipped wine from her golden cup and then transferred it to Aocao's mouth. Aroused by their felicitous intimacy, two white deer and two dancing cranes in the garden also mated, pressing their hind quarters against each other. Everyone observing the scene secretly tittered. The empress, however, paid little attention, as though she and her lover were alone in the world.

One night they slept a sound sleep, their naked limbs entangled with each other, after their excessive immersion in sensual pleasure. They did not rise until the sun was high in the sky.

"Lord of Perfect Satisfaction," said the empress when she arose, "you could not have had so happy an encounter even if you had graduated the state examinations with the highest honors, and had been appointed Prime Minister. You have served me with heart and soul, and in return I have given you the privilege of enjoying the delicacies and raiment provided only to the monarch. No one can say I am not kind to you. I could even have ennobled you but for your adamant rejection, but I am willing to honor your brothers or your other relatives by promoting them to positions of eminence. I promise you that I will never go back on my word."

"I have told Your Majesty before that I have neither family nor siblings," said Aocao. "Since my meteoric rise has not been due to my personal talent, I am not very interested in titles or wealth. What I am concerned about is only one thing, which I shall tell Your Majesty despite the fact that you might be unwilling to hear it, and might therefore execute me. Still, I beg Your Majesty's indulgence. Nothing could honor me more than your willingness to incline your ear to what I am about to say to you. Even though my words cost me my life, I can have no fear of facing the consequences."

"Tut, tut!" chided the empress. "You should not utter such words so inauspicious, Lord of Perfect Satisfaction! You are my heart and soul, so how could I not listen to you?"

"I appreciate very much your kind respect ," said Aocao.

"For what reason was the Prince of Luling demoted and banished to the remoteness of Fangzhou? Did he commit a serious crime? Moreover, and to my knowledge, he has lately been mending his ways. Should people misunderstand your intentions, and come to believe that you wish to destroy the Tang Royal House, is it not likely that after you are gone, the same disaster visited on the clan of Empress Lu[92] will befall your own?" People are not yet wearied of the Tang dynasty. In my humble opinion, the Prince of Luling should be summoned back to the capital and reinstated. Your Majesty is of noble character and enjoys lofty prestige and universal respect. What other happiness can be compared with this?"[93]

The empress hesitated.

"Royal Majesty," Aocao went on, "if my petition grates upon on your ear, I shall have no choice but to castrate myself. This is the only way I can make my apology to your people."

He seized a knife and plunged it into his genitals. Though the knife was swiftly snatched away by the Empress, the head of his organ had already been injured, the cut about half an inch deep and bleeding badly. The empress immediately fetched a clean cloth and wiped the blood dry. When she breathed on the wound to warm it, she could not help weeping.[94]

---

92 Empress Lu, after the death of her son, Emperor Hui, enfeoffed a number of her relatives and installed them in the most important offices of state. This was universally seen as a move destroy the Han dynasty, and after she died, they, together with numerous members of the Lu clan, were slaughtered. For details, see Sima Qian, *Shi ji* (Records of the Grand Historian), vol. 2, pp. 395–412.

93 Historically, it was the high official, Di Renjie, rather than Xue Huaiyi, (the alter-ego of Aocao), who persuaded Empress Wu to summon the Prince of Luling back to the capital.

94 According to the official histories of the Tang, it was suggested more than once that Xue Huaiyi should be castrated since he spent so much time inside the palace supervising the

"Oh my very silly son!" she scolded him, in tears. "How could you do such a stupid thing!"

"I am not your real son," said Aocao. "You might take me as your temporary son, yet I cannot replace your legitimate offspring who is your own flesh and blood. You really cannot abandon him."

The empress vacillated.

Henceforward, Aocao would seek every opportunity to repeat his admonitions until the Prince of Luling, with the strong backing of Lord Di [Renjie], had been summoned back and restored to his former position as Heir Apparent. Those who had resented Aocao for his illicit relationship with the Empress and had long been harboring an intent to assassinate him, changed their attitude and praised him to the sky as soon as they heard of his urgings to re-establish the Tang dynasty.

It was now the second year of the Yuantong reign-title,[95] and Empress Wu was seventy-six years old. She often felt indisposed, and her daily diet was accordingly reduced. One day she said to Aocao, "Many a year has passed since first we met. Although we have taken great joy in each other's company, our bliss cannot last much longer. My health is now rapidly declining and I worry constantly about your situation."

"I would not have dared to bring this matter up had Your Majesty not mentioned it," he said. "Sexual intemperance is detrimental to well-being and Your Majesty might thereafter have to abstain from overindulgence in order to maintain your health. You have now reached a venerable age. Should you in the fullness of time depart this world, then I, your humble servant, would surely have no reason not to follow you. I care little about my own body, I must assure you, but I fret deeply that my corporeal coarseness might profane your holy spirit."

"Do not worry," said the empress. "I shall arrange a way for you."

Several days later she said to him, "Here is my plan for you. My dearly-beloved nephew Wu Chengsi, Prince of Wei, is very kind. You may find refuge at his residence. Once you learn that I have passed away, change your name and flee. With all your money, and the treasures I have given you, it should be very easy for you to find in the South or in the Southwest a comfortable abode for yourself."

The next day, she summoned Wu Chengsi.

---

construction of the Hall of Light. The empress ignored these petitions.

95 The fictitious second year of Yuantong corresponds historically to the second year of Shengli, i.e., 699.

"You know my relationship with Xue Aocao," she said to him. "I love you more than any of my own sons and today I entrust him to you. Let him take refuge at your home and treat him graciously. Do not intervene shoud he wish to venture out, but exercise great care. Should outsiders learn of his sojourn with you, you are bound to suffer numerous troubles."

Wu Chengsi was shocked.

"I will do as you say!" he replied.

That evening, Empress Wu gave a farewell banquet in honor of Aocao. Displayed on the table were delicacies from land and sea, including fetus of leopard, hump of camel, tail of red goat, dried meat of green snail, as well as a variety of the most renowned wine paid to the Tang Imperial House as tribute by the surrounding vassal states, such as Xiliang in the west and Thailand in the south. The Empress, holding high her golden goblet studded with seven precious objects, toasted Aocao, and her *sotto voce* murmurings, intermingled with sobs, accompanied each cup she drained. In return Aocao drank his fill, and as he became intoxicated he could not help weeping, too.

"Royal Majesty," he sobbed, "from this moment onward, I shall never again hear the tinkle of your jewelry nor the jingling of your trinkets. Take good care of yourself, and be sure to eat whatever nutritious foodstuffs your appetite will allow. I am so very, very sorry that I have not been able to complete my duty of service to you. Should you still have need of me after your ascension into Heaven, may your spirit descend again and find me waiting at your bedside..."

His words unfinished, the empress was already drowning in tears, weeping and wailing loudly, incapable of uttering a single word.

"Lord of Perfect Satisfaction," she said when she had finally calmed, "I appreciate your deep affection for an old woman who is now on the verge of death. I have heard that it is a popular custom among those who secretly love each other to brand a scar on the lover's skin. How wonderfully romantic it must be! Perhaps you and I should follow suit?"

The empress ordered her servants to fetch some ambergris, and after swearing an oath and twice bowing to Heaven, placed her brand on the head of Aocao's penis. Then she burned the same brand at a spot on her own pudenda.

"It was in pain that I started my relationship with you," she said, "and in pain it is now coming to its end. How marvelous!"

Then they retired to the bedchamber.

The empress said to him, "No regret in my life has been more painful than my separation from you. Tonight I must indulge my pleasure to the very fullest! I wish only that I could die drowning in such joy!"

At her bidding, Aocao repeated, one by one, each and every one of the varied games of love they had earlier played, transported as they had been, in voluptuous joy. In each posture, the empress would accept at least ten of his thrusts, and by the dawn of the next day, they were both utterly exhausted, splayed out in bed like two corpses.

That day, the Empress had three hundred catties of gold, a peck of pearls, a large quantity of coral and jade, and fifty suits of male attire prepared for Aocao, and had them loaded on a cart and sent to Chengsi's residence.

She said to Chengsi after Aocao had taken his tearful leave, "Take good care of Master Xue just as if you were taking good care of me!"

Chengsi did his utmost, day and night, to be a hospitable host. He feasted Aocao as frequently as possible, and at each banquet would have his favorite concubine Wen Boxiang raise his spirits with her beautiful singing. Boxiang had been a famous courtesan in Chang'an before becoming the concubine of Chengsi, and she became so smitten with Aocao's manly beauty and virility that she would ogle him whenever she could. One night she crept into his bedchamber in the hope of making love with him, yet however hard she tried to force his huge penis into herself, succeeded only in moistening the tip. Embarrassed, she bit him on the shoulder and left.

After recovering from her illness, Empress Wu gradually regained her health. She was now able to stroll slowly around in the rear courtyard, and one day she had a feast laid out in the garden to entertain the Zhang brothers. She was deeply impressed by their extraordinary beauty and talent, and her loving affection for them was re-kindled.

She summoned Changzong into the palace.

"For the past few years I seem to have been possessed by spirits, and have forgotten your very existence until today," she said.

Changzong did not dare to question the truth of her explanation, but after they re-commenced their intercourse, he was surprised to find that her vagina was much looser than before. For her part, the Empress experienced a similar shock at how small his penis seemed. Without passion, they both persisted in their engagement, and neither of them reached satisfaction. The empress then summoned Yizhi, and he, too, failed to provide the gratification she desired.

A month later, she sent a young eunuch to Chengsi's residence to secretly give Aocao a small package which contained a shining pearl, ten red love-beads, a hundred pieces of ambergris, and a pair of mandarin ducks in colors of gold and purple. When he opened the package, he found a letter inside, written on gold-flecked paper watermarked with figures of flying dragons and dancing phoenixes. It read as follows:

Since our too-hasty parting, nothing has made me feel a more lively regret than your loss. Flowers in the morning see me drink alone, and the moon at night witnesses my solitary slumber. Neither do I want for maidens beautiful nor youths handsome around me. Yet I find myself bereft of a true lover in whose company I can take delight. My tears have become my constant companions, leaving their stains from moment to moment on my clothing and on my desk. Oh! How joyful I was in the past! And how joyless my world now! How short were the days of former times! And how long they seem of late! After our too-brief farewell we have been torn apart, like the cleavage between Heaven and earth. So close together we dwell, yet are no longer able to touch, as though we lived in lands far, far away from each other. Life is too fleeting to endure the suffering of separation like this! Today I write to you in the hope that you might return to me for a brief reunion. I shall send for you on the night when the moon is full. Conceal yourself in the ox-cart I shall provide, and enter the palace through the Gate of Spring. Our predestined love has yet to fully run its course, and some days of sojourn in the palace might perhaps establish a new intimacy which will be rekindled in our next incarnation. Fail not to keep the appointed time. Should you take for granted that I will be in the company of someone else, and therefore decline to meet with me, I would be desolated. Pray, bring this letter with you when you come, for I shall await you.

She had attached a poem to the letter:

Are the colors green and red different or the same?
I cannot tell as the state of my mind is insane.
My cheeks sallow, and my body in ruins,
I am pining for you, and only you, in vain.
Oh, should you disbelieve that the tears on my face,
Have been constant since you moved away,
Come and find evidence in my storage closet,
Where on my dresses is still left their trace.

Aocao, before even having read the letter through, burst into tears. Since the young eunuch was waiting outside for his reply, he had to apply himself to its composition without delay, and no sooner had the letter been completed than he handed it to the messenger, who departed immediately.

Now, with no one around him, he heaved a sigh.

"If I return," he debated with himself, "I shall never be able to leave again. I must be circumspect. People say that we have two sovereigns, and how true it is! How fortunate for me that I have removed myself from the palace!"

That night he took a small portion of his gold and treasure, and riding on a fleet steed that he had stolen from Chengsi's stable, he fled. Stealthily, he rode out through the Western Gate and not until much later was Chengsi aware of his escape.

Surprised, Chengsi dispatched at once his cavalry to search for him in every possible hiding-place in the surrounding regions, but without success. He was then obliged to report his disappearance to the empress, begging for punishment. The empress said nothing, though she was devastated.

Changzong, learning of the empress' unhappiness, spent ten thousand ounces of gold to purchase the special Nanhai elixirs renowned for their ability to enlarge a man's endowment, and for a full month or so, he and Yizhi ingested the tonics they had to raise their "turtles".[96] In due course they entered the palace, ready to resume their sexual services.

Both brothers, in the last year of her reign, were murdered by the Heir Apparent and Prime Minister Zhang Jianzhi[97] in a surprise attack, and their bodies were dismembered just outside the empress' bedchamber.

The Heir Apparent, after his enthronement, honored Aocao and sought everywhere to find him, but his search was fruitless.

Many years later, in the Tianbao reign-period when Xuanzong[98] was on the throne, someone reportedly saw Aocao in the city of Chengdu,[99] wearing a robe made of feathers and a cap of yellow.[100] His complexion was ruddy and his hair black, so that he appeared still to be in his twenties. People said that he had attained to unity with the *Dao*.

No one, however, has been able to discover anything of his later life, nor when he died.

Postscript

History needs romances just as the Classics need commentary. What is unclear in the classics, annotations explain, and what is unsaid in history, romances complement.

Detailed descriptions of the boudoir in the stories of Emperor Wu of the Han dynasty, or of [Zhao] Feiyan[101] reveal dimensions that are only vaguely mentioned in the historical records; and modern readers would surely find these tales as helpful in understanding history as they find annotations useful in their study of the Classics.

Recently, I found myself in possession of a copy of *Lord of Perfect Satisfaction*. As I was reading it, I was deeply impressed by its meticulous and

---

96 Penis.

97 Zhang Jianzhi was a protégé of Di Renjie, and was the ringleader of the 705 coup which deposed the empress.

98 Xuanzong, the third son of Li Dan, Emperor Ruizong (r. 710–712) was on the throne from 712-756. The Tianbao Reign refers to the years between 742 and 756.

99 Chengdu is in Sichuan province, in southwestern China, a center of Daoism since the Han dynasty.

100 The typical garb of a Daoist priest or adept.

101 The reference here is to "*Han Wudi neizhuan*" (Inner Chronicle of Emperor Wu of the Han Dynasty) and "*Feiyan waizhuan*" (An Unofficial History of Zhao Feiyan).

lifelike narration and description, which, I should say, are far more entertaining than any other historical romances I have read. For this reason, I have decided to publish it so that other interested readers may also enjoy the delights of this splendid piece of work.

Liu Bosheng[102]

102 This is a pseudonym, and the real identity of the writer is unknown.

MEMOIR OF A CRAZY OLD WOMAN

Preface

What is passion?

Passion is human nature stirred. Human nature, which reveals itself in the form of passion as it is stirred up, is actually the embodiment of mind. If mind is not upright, human nature deviates, and when it deviates it is no longer restrained and controllable. Guided by a mind which is filled with desires and lacking restraint, passion will burst out, incontinent.

This can be seen especially in the bedchamber.

I have observed women of great passion. At the outset, their passion was no more than a single errant thought. However, once they pursued their inclinations, their desires knew no bounds. Some of them fell deeply in love with men who were much older or younger or who were related to them, or were their servants or clergymen. Insane with passion, they indulged themselves in carnal pleasure with no sense of shame or moral principle. There were none, however, who were not deeply regretful of their misconduct as their passion faded and their beauty no longer fascinated. Alas! Had they exercised self-control beforehand, they would have suffered no chagrin; had they made love within their conjugal confines rather than indulging in illicit liaisons with a collection of men from outside their marriage, they would not have stained their family reputation.

Thus, I suggest that girls be taught to restrain their minds when they are young, in order to curb their desires in advance and to preclude any surrender to passion. When their minds are upright and their passion is contained, where would one find even one of those laughing stocks—the lewd female?

Tiaolangyue -1764

Memoir of a Crazy Old Woman[1]

In a dilapidated town in Zheng-Wei[2] there lives an elderly woman, seventy years old, white-haired, and toothless. She dwells on a small narrow street and loves talking about her past, never feeling fatigued with her long hours of prattling reminiscences.

Enjoying the privilege of visiting notables of the local region, she, one day at the residence of a dignitary, encountered a person by the name of Yan Qiongke,[3] who curiously inquired:

"My respected elder, in spite of your hunched back and your use of a staff, I can tell from your elegant manner and your graceful bearing that you must have been a beauty when you were young. As a person from a younger generation, however, I know nothing of your life. Now that I have fortuitously made your acquaintance, a charming lady of an advanced age, I wish you to grant me an opportunity to listen to your stories. It would be my greatest pleasure should you honor my request."

The old woman laughed.

"How would I dare to relate to you my unworthy personal history if you were not so interested?" she said. "Now that you have made this request, I am afraid I have no choice but to accede."

"I shall write down the stories you are about to relate," said Qiongke.

---

1 The word *chi* in the title (rendered as "crazy") is hard to translate, for in the story it means both "silly" and "crazily passionate," and there is no English equivalent that can completely cover both the meanings.

2 Zheng-Wei, abbreviations of the State of Zheng and the State of Wei of the Zhou dynasty, are located in present-day Henan province. For their exact locations in Zhou dynasty, see Gao Heng, *Shijing jinzhu* (Contemporary Annotation of the Book of Poetry), pp.7–8. Zheng-Wei is also a metaphor for a part of early China where lewdness was rife.

3 The name, Yan Qiongke, is neutral in gender, and in fact, stands for the author herself. As suggested in the Introduction, Yan Qiongke and Madame Hibiscus are the same person, and the protagonist of the story, Shangguan Enuo is essentially relating her story to herself.

The old woman, dressed in plain clothing, raised herself slightly from her seat, her hand pressed to the front part of her garb and her long sleeves drooping.

"I am old and have one foot already in the grave," she said with a smile. "Knowing that my body is soon to moulder like dead grasses, I find the romances I experienced in my youth especially precious. It would be regrettable if I were to let them sink into oblivion!"

My surname was Tang, a family which had originally been a branch of the clan of Shangguan but later had been severed from it. This is the reason why I have now adopted the surname Shangguan, though in fact, I do not really belong to any branch of the Shangguan family. My father's given-name was Ji and my mother's name was He Lian. She bore only two daughters. I was the elder one, named Enuo, and her second daughter, my younger sister, was called Xianjuan.

I can still recall when, at the age of seven or eight, my sister and I were playing in the courtyard when my father asked each of us to improvise a poem on the blooming plum-trees. I composed a couplet:

They are not vying for glamour after the snow,
Yet toward the moon are smiling with allure.[4]

My father was angry. "In the future, she may become a wanton woman!" he said.

My sister also composed a couplet:

They are not so beautiful as the scene of a deep valley,
But like the spring in the Shanglin Park are appealing.[5]

Smiling, my mother commented, "If Enuo turns out to be what she describes in her poem, she may end up only as a beauteous "flower girl."[6] Xianjuan is modest, and she will not go astray."

From the age of twelve or thirteen, I no longer cut my hair. I would have it loosely dressed into a bun and would often pace to and fro in front of a mirror, looking at myself with admiration.

---

4 In Chinese literature, snow usually stands for chastity, whereas the "moon" (*yue*) can be understood as a part of the phrase *fengyue* (breeze and moon), which is a euphemism for prostitution.

5 The second line refers to a famous *fu* composition by Sima Xiangru of the Han period that describes in great detail the imperial hunting park, the Shanglin yuan.

6 The term "flower girl" refers to a courtesan.

"How fortunate you are to have your parents think so highly[7] of you!" I sighed one day to my younger sister. "Life is short, and how foolish we would be to wait for the Yellow River to run clear before seeking pleasures of our own."[8]

"Elder Sister, what would you have me do?" my sister responded with a smile to my complaint. "You are not fifteen yet, so why not join our cousins at cockfighting or football?"

It had been years since I had studied the poems of the Zhou dynasty.[9] My parents forbade me to recite them because of their erotic nature,[10] so I read them silently and secretly without their knowledge. Though at the beginning, I was rather confused about the descriptions of love between male and female, I later attained some understanding. I said to myself, "What is described in those poems is simply the relationship like that which I have seen between Mother and Father. The only difference is that they make love in private while those poems of love describe activities which take place in plain sight of everyone."

However, I still knew nothing of the pleasures that people in love enjoyed. How is it that a "sly lad" makes a girl forget to eat and sleep[11] and a "gentleman" comes to see a lady in the early morning 'when wind and rain are chill'"?[12] Why does a woman toss a peach to her beloved man in order to receive his reply,[13] and another wish to conceal herself with a stranger amid

---

7 The original Chinese text for "think so highly" is "*xiangcui*," meaning "fragrant and crisp," which does not make sense in the context. It is obviously a mistake and has therefore been corrected in the translation. There are some other errors like this in the original text and they have also been corrected in the translation.

8 This idiom comes originally from *Zuo's Commentary on Spring and Autumn Annals*. The Yellow River has always been muddy, so to wait for it to run clear would be hopeless.

9 "Poems of the Zhou dynasty" refer to the poems in *Shijing* (The Book of Poetry), the earliest collection of Chinese verses, and one of the five Confucian Classics which formed the core of the traditional Chinese education system. The collection consists of 305 poems, divided into four sections-the Airs of the States, the Greater and Lesser Elegantiae, and the Hymns. The 160 poems of the Airs of the States, in which we find the *Zheng* and *Wei* sections, take as their subject, the daily experiences of ordinary people, and often deal with sexual love and its attendant emotions. The best known translations are those by James Legge, Arthur Waley, Bernard Kalgren and Ezra Pound.

10 Some of the poems offer allusive, though rather explicit accounts of love-making, such as number 23, "...There is a girl who longs for spring/A fine fellow seduces her...Oh, undress me slowly/Oh, do not disturb my kerchief...."

11 The reference is to the poem "*Jiaotong*" (Sly Lad) in the *Zheng* section of *The Book of Poetry*.

12 The reference is to the poem "*Fengyu* " (Wind and Rain) in the *Zheng* section of *The Book of Poetry*.

13 The reference is to the poem "*Mugua*" (Papaya) in the *Wei* section of *The Book of Poetry*.

the grass when she "meets him by chance"?[14] Is it an exaggeration to say that "one day seems like three months" when a maiden cannot meet her sweetheart?[15]

I really did not understand.

A young married woman living on the north side of our house was sexually experienced and I consulted her one day when she was unoccupied.

"Man and woman are different," I said. "But why does a man called Mang miss a woman so much as to cross the River Wei and the River Zhen to see her?[16] A man may take the trouble to simulate a fox, naked, in order to court a woman he loves;[17] but if he does not love her, can she love someone else?[18] Does the description of a 'sly lad' and a woman's love for him suggest that she is intoxicated with him for no reason at all, or does it refer to that loving affection which is most profound?"[19]

"You are not married yet," replied the young woman, "so you should not ask these questions."

"It is precisely because I am unmarried that I have these questions," I said. "Can a woman go to a man's home and rashly declare, 'We are husband and wife'? Why does she not seize a man on the road and call him 'my husband'?"

"Young lady, it seems that you are reaching maturity," said the young woman. "Are you now harboring thoughts of love and pining for a handsome young man to seduce you? Well, let me tell you the difference between men and women. A man is the same as a woman so far as his ears, eyes, nose, mouth, and limbs are concerned. The difference lies at the base of his belly and between his thighs, where there is a thing at once supple and hard, able both to contract and to extend, its shape like a pestle or a spear, or like a snail. That thing we call the 'penis.' Beneath it is a part that looks like a warrior holding a spear or a sheath containing a sharp weapon. That part is called the 'scrotum'".

I was amazed.

"I have no such a thing below my belly and between my thighs!" I said.

---

14 The reference is to the poem "*Yeyou Mancao*" (Wild Grass in the Wilderness) in the *Zheng* section of *The Book of Poetry*.

15 The reference is to the poem "Zejin" (A Man's Garments) in the *Zheng* section of *The Book of Poetry*.

16 The reference is to the poem "*Mang*" in the *Wei* section of *The Book of Poetry*.

17 The reference is to the poem "*Youhu*" (Fox) in the *Wei* section of *The Book of Poetry*.

18 The reference is to the poem "*Qianshang*" (Open the Clothing) in the *Zheng* section of *The Book of Poetry*.

19 The reference is to the poem "Sly Lad" in *The Book of Poetry*.

"That is what makes men different from women," the young woman explained. "You and I as women are endowed with female sexual parts, which, located below our girdle and at the inner sides of the crotch of our trousers, resemble a clam if viewed at a distance or appear to be a split melon when gazed upon closely. In comparison with the male organ hanging between their thighs and extending outward as it becomes erect, we find that our private parts have only an entrance passage and have no protruding bulge. That is how women are endowed by nature."

"They have something superfluous whereas we lack something," I wondered. "But that difference is not enough to resolve my doubts as to why men and women find so much pleasure in loving each other."

"Well, I can perhaps only enlighten you by ascribing it to the will of Heaven," said the young woman. "In the primordial ages, men and women, though created different, lived together in the caves they had built. They wore bark and leaves as clothing in winter to protect themselves from the freezing cold. But when summer came and the heat was sweltering, they would remove their bark and leaves, so that they were stark naked. As they walked about, unashamed in their nakedness, they saw their different female and male forms, one being concave and the other convex. The convexity of a man, when following the impulse of *yang*, would become tumescent and virile, and would therefore be able to enter into a woman's concavity if they happened to meet in passing. The man might have been astonished by her lack of the same protruding organ; and certainly did not know that his entry into her would open the gate to perpetual reproduction, create endless life, plant the root of lust, and germinate the sprout of love. After he entered into her, he would feel so pleasing a sensation that he could not refrain from repeating his movements. Believing that her concavity was no more than a grotto to be penetrated, he would keep pumping with great enthusiasm. The more he pumped, the more pleasure he would feel, and the titillating sensations would prompt him to repeat his motions ceaselessly until at last a jolt of delight would race down his spine to his groin, making his secretions flow out. His emissions would provide him with such ecstasy that he would be unable to contain his joy. He would then tell other men about his experience; and that is how men and women came to take pleasure with each other."

"Really?" I said, dubiously. "Was this really how men and women began to love each other?"

"Well, what I have told you is simply my own surmise," said the young woman. "Yet the real circumstances were probably not so very different. The difference is simply that at first, the entry of a man's convexity into a woman's concavity would usually hurt the woman rather than give her pleasure."

"If that is the case," I inquired, "what is the source of the delight?"

"Delight has something to do with the size of a man's convexity," said the young woman. "The larger it is, the more it will hurt a woman in their initial intercourse. A woman cannot receive a man with comfort until after her pain dissipates; then she will enjoy a delightful feeling, so wondrous that I find words incapable of describing it. As for a convexity of small size, it may not make a woman suffer much, but it will not bring her much pleasure either."

I became even more bewildered.

"Why does pleasure come from pain and why will there be no pleasure if there is no pain?" I asked.

"The female concavity," said the young woman, "is like the bud of a lotus ready to burst, very tight and dry the first time it allows a man entrance. Even a tiny convexity may hurt it, not to mention a huge one."

"Then how can a woman experience pleasure?"

"Inside her concavity," explained the young woman, "there is a part shaped like a fleshy bud-like tongue, and as it slightly extends to touch the tip of the man's stiffened convex object, the woman will feel so tingly that a sense of rapturous pleasure will gradually overcome her pain and become dominant. This sense of delight will be lacking if the man's object is short and small, unable to reach the female part in question. So you must ensure that you find one that is large, lengthy, and firm, capable of filling every corner of your interior space and able to prod and churn about forcefully in it. You must first endure the wear and tear of coupling until you feel you are eager and ablaze inside. Then an ecstatic delight will flow over you."

The young woman had hardly completed her explanation when, suddenly, I felt a faint thrill in my loins.

I quickly took leave of her and went back home, filled with a desire to try out this experience with a man. I did meet a youth when I was returning home, but did not find him to be the type I liked. With no other recourse, I secluded myself in a hidden spot, and inserted my finger into my vagina, stroking it for some time with my head bent down. Despite a sensation of arousal, my desires went unsatisfied.

A younger cousin of mine by the name of Huimin, who had come to our home to study with my parents, was at the time living with us. He was lodged in an outer chamber. As a youth in his teens, he was strikingly virile and handsome, and finding him desirable, I could not help taking a fancy to him.

One day, Mother and Father were both away. I invited Huimin to amuse himself with my sister and me. As we gathered around our bed, Huimin took hold of my sister's arm insisting that they have a contest of the strength. My sister vied with him, and for a long while he could not best her. Seeing that the night was getting late, I stopped them.

"Hey!" I said. "You two have been amusing yourself all day. Are you not yet tired? It is now time to go to sleep, and you'd better give up your contest for today. Huimin, you may sleep in our bed with us if you wish."

"He is a boy!" said my younger sister. "How can he sleep with us?"

"I am afraid of ghosts," said Huimin. "I want to share the bed with you."

I persuaded my sister, saying, "He is too young to know about anything except food and clothing. You need not unduly concern yourself."

We then undressed and slept, with my sister taking the outer side of the bed, me in the middle, and Huimin occupying the inner section. Exhausted, he soon dropped off. As I was unable to fall asleep, I stealthily caressed his belly and found that there was indeed something convex at its base, precisely as the young woman had described. The object, however, was very small.

"How can such a puny thing do me harm?" I said to myself. "If I seduce him into inserting it into me, I shall have a taste of how it feels in my body, and with such an experience I shall no longer fear a man's member. Why should I care about its small size? I must do it with him tonight!"

Once again I stroked Huimin's object and felt that it had become hard and erect. Moreover, it was unyielding despite its smallness. I was excited, shaking him until he woke up, and then took his hand and guided it to my private parts.

He chuckled.

"Elder Sister,"[20] he whispered, "it's weird that yours is like that."

Without replying, I seized his hard, swollen erection with one hand and turned sideways toward him. I then used my other hand to embrace him and twist his body to make him turn around. Under my direction, his hard, swollen object moved closer to me and was finally placed against my vulva.

"What are you doing, Elder Sister?" he asked.

"I want you to put it into me," I replied in a low voice.

"What for?" he asked, rather confused.

"Do what I told you and do not ask," I said. "Just slip it into me hard."

Huimin did as I asked, his penis surging forward with all its strength through my hand and into my private quarters. But it missed the middle of the entryway and battered only the urethra above. This was not where it should go. To make it enter the right channel I twisted my body over him. The adjustment, however, left my entry a little too low for him. I then turned

---

20 Cousins usually addressed each other as brother and sister as a sign of affection and respect.

around with my back toward him so that he could penetrate me from behind. Still he was unable to find the right portal no matter how I adjusted my posture to meet him.

"I think I must lie on my back," I said.

I lay on my back and drew him onto me. It was only when he renewed his efforts that I found my gateway was still too distant for his object to reach. I then parted my thighs to let him squeeze into the space between, and meanwhile, my hand guided him to the right orifice.

"Here you go," I said. "This is where you should enter."

"Good!" he said, trying to drive it all the way up.

I felt a sharp pain.

"Stop!" I cried.

As he ceased his movements, I began to think that the pain was not intolerable though it did hurt me to a considerable extent. I then asked him to resume his exertions. This time, however, I felt a stabbing twinge as though I were being stung by needles.

His penis chafed, Huimin seemed also to feel some discomfort.

"Elder Sister," he complained, frowning, "why are you obliging me to do something so distressing? I find you very dry inside and my soreness seems to be caused by the dryness. What should I do?"

"Rest for a moment, then," I said.

I stroked and kneaded his organ with my hand. It was only about half an inch longer than my finger, with no skin on the tip, and its head felt as if there were a ridge surrounding it. I was amazed at its form. For some reason, it seemed difficult to force its entry into me.

Suddenly having an idea, I suggested, "Spit some saliva onto it, so that it will no longer be dry."

Huimin spat as I had suggested, and surprisingly, this did help him cleave more smoothly into me. Despite my excitement at the confirmation of my hearsay knowledge that saliva was useful in opening a tight vagina, I felt that I had been inflicted with a massive, burning pain as I was filled to the point of bursting. It was a suffering far more intense than I had ever felt before.

"Stop moving!" I screamed.

"With spittle I am able to enter without difficulty," he said. "Why do you want me to stop?"

"Too painful to bear," I gasped.

"Then you shouldn't have urged me to do this in the first place," he grumbled.

"Well, you have been stabbing me too hard," I said. "You should pump instead."

"What do you mean by 'pump'?" he asked.

"To 'pump'," I explained, "is to partially withdraw your object and then push it back in, keeping each repeated motion well inside me."

He then began to practice the pumping motion, exploring this technique for a long while. But for me, the pain seemed even more unbearable.

"Go more slowly." I groaned.

At my request, Huimin did slow down slightly, though it was not of much help in alleviating my affliction. What was worse, I began to feel suffocated as if I were being choked by food in my throat.

I found the experience far from enjoyable.

"Elder Sister," he panted, "you urged me to "pump," and now that object of mine is becoming very tingly."

I was skeptical.

"How does it happen that he is titillated whereas I am not?" I mused. "Could it be that the young woman deceived me?"

"Leave me alone for a moment," I said. "I am not really comfortable with you churning around in there so violently."

"But it makes me feel so good," he said. "Please, please allow me to continue."

The pain in my vagina was incessant and I was so distressed that I wished I could bring him to a halt immediately. He, however, rammed forward against me even harder than before.

"Oh, what pleasure!" he exclaimed. "I feel ecstatic."

His member was only two inches long, about the size of my index finger, yet with only an inch inside me, it still felt excruciating! This further convinced me that even if it was small, a man's endowment could be rather difficult to admit for the first time.

Before long my sister turned and woke up. Hastily, I pushed him off. Huimin lay down quickly pretending to be still asleep. After some while, he rose to use the chamber pot, and when he was finished, I saw that his object had become shrunken like a dead silkworm, no longer of a lively and vigorous appearance.

Giggling, I said, "My sister is awake. Won't you feel embarrassed if she sees you?"

"Elder Sister," he exclaimed in a whisper, "you have enlightened me on affairs of which I was previously ignorant, and you have tutored me with patience. Now that my passions are aroused, I should like continue my lessons with you forever!"

"But no more tonight, silly boy!" I said. "You may visit again tomorrow evening."

I bolstered his head with my arm as we fell asleep. His long hair, which already reached his brows, felt quite thick and prickly to the touch of my arm and bosom.

The next day Huimin spoke to his fellow students at the private school he attended. "Last night I slept with my elder sister and she compelled me to penetrate her with my prick. At her request, I entered her and then pulled out and entered her again, over and over, like a monk who is royally drunk, staggering in and out of the temple gate."

"Your sister seduced you because she wanted you to be inside her," remarked a fellow student. "If you had continued to hump her for a longer time she would have become wet inside and you would have been able to shove yourself in, all the way to the hilt."

That evening my sister and I were ready for bed when Huimin came into our chamber again. "Huimin," said my sister, "last night when you shared our bed, you disturbed me so much that you kept me awake for the greater part of the night! Tonight I must drive you back to your own room to sleep."

"He disturbed you," I interjected, "simply because he could not sleep well and tried to adjust himself to a new bed. I am certain that he will not toss and turn tonight as he did last night."

"Elder Sister," said Huimin, "I had no anxieties last night with you sleeping beside me. If you are as considerate as you were yesterday, and continue to let me spend the night here, I would be most grateful!"

"But I can't sleep comfortably with him glued to us," my sister said, disgruntled.

"Yes you can," he argued.

Finally, the three of us ended up sharing the bed once more. My sister, who was unwilling to squeeze against us head to head, moved her pillow to the other end of the bed.

Huimin had no sooner crawled under the quilt than both his hands began an assault between my legs. I resisted his invasion for fear that my sister, who had not yet closed her eyes, might discover our intimacy. He then stimulated his organ with his hand until it achieved erection.

"Now lie on your back. Please!" he begged me. "I can no longer contain myself."

"But you gave me not an iota of pleasure yesterday," I said with my back to him. "Why should I indulge you again?"

His impatience grew even greater.

"You are the one who inveigled me into sleeping with you," he muttered. "If I were to engage you from behind, you might feel an even greater discomfort!"

There seemed to be no alternative for me but to draw him upon me once again.

Before thrusting forward, Huimin spat on his penis. This time my passage was moist and his entry seemed so much easier that I felt scarcely any pain. As he grew more and more violent, however, and punched against that portion of me which had previously been intact, I was once more seized in throes of torment; and since he refused to halt his thrusts even for a moment out of sympathy for my intolerable pain, I had to grab onto his instrument to stop any further penetration. In a frenzy of desire, Huimin disregarded my attempt to obstruct him and jabbed at me even harder than before, until he had buried his object entirely inside me, leaving not an inch outside.

In agony, I could not help cursing, "Why are you so impetuous, you wretch?"

"I am sure you know," he said, "that a general in the field is not bound by orders from his sovereign."

I had no one but myself to blame.

"Why am I angry?" I said to myself. "Why did I ask for it the first time, and then ask for it again?"

He began his pounding again.

"Careful," I warned him, "go forward only half an inch at a time and don't be precipitate!"

He drove himself into me, and each time, he would push all the way to the root regardless of some scratchy resistance. It was really torture for me! Fortunately, his member was neither bulky nor lengthy in size, and after some while, and in spite of a wretched and disagreeable feeling, I gradually became accustomed to it.

He then speeded up his movements.

"How dare you assault me so fiercely without my permission?" I gasped.

In spite of my protests, he refused to stop his lunges.

Two hundred strokes later, his member suddenly became hot and tingly and he felt unable to contain the discharge of his "urine." Although I resented him for his rapid motions, as his object engorged and filled the entire centre of my vagina, my pain seemed to lessen a little.

"Take it out," I said, nevertheless. "You are torturing me!"

Huimin took no notice, and thrust into me even more energetically. Unable to endure the suffering, I was on the verge of crying.

"Oh, it is so painful!" I groaned. "It is as if you are tearing me apart. I can't bear it any longer!"

Still ignoring my entreaties, he continued violently to thrust and pound away. For fear that my sister would discover what was taking place between us,

I could only stifle my anguish and suffer silently. Resentfully, I chewed on my quilt, feeling deeply disgruntled.

Suddenly he burst out, "Oh, God! Oh, God! What is this strange and tingling quiver washing over my whole body? It is rising from my very root to engulf my entire frame! I am frightened. Something is about to explode deep inside me."

I was intrigued, and soon I did feel some sort of fluid inundating my insides. A delightful sensation, neither long-lasting nor completely prevailing over the pain that had been afflicting me, coursed throughout my body. In the meantime, moans and groans escaped from Huimin's mouth; and then all of sudden, his entire torso collapsed upon me. In my painful wretchedness, however, I could not bring myself to move an inch and could only embrace him tightly.

After a while I asked him, "What has happened to you?"

"I don't know," he gasped. "Even now, I still feel too limp to lift my body. It feels as though it weighs a thousand pounds. How excessive the pleasure was!"

I broke into a grin.

"How fortunate for you that your bliss was so great!" I said. "I myself felt no delight at all. Since the suffering never left me, how could I expect to feel enjoyment?"

I carefully lowered him down onto the bed. Though he was no longer inside me, the distasteful sensation in my vagina still remained, as if something internal had been permanently lost. Moreover, this disagreeable sensation seemed to be accompanied by a sense of burning heat, reminding me that I had not yet reached satisfaction.

But his member was no longer powerful and vigorous. I swabbed it clean with my handkerchief and then wiped myself dry. With our legs intertwined we embraced each other as we prepared to sleep.

We had fallen deeply in love.

"Although I experienced no pleasure," I whispered to Huimin, "it was not your fault."

After having tasted the delights of intercourse, Huimin glued himself to me from morning to night.

One evening, the moon shone brightly and I dragged him out for a walk. I held his arm as we ambled along, and he took liberties with me, slipping one hand into my crotch. Since we had been so intimate, I could do nothing more than allow him to fondle me as much as he liked.

Later that night, upon his insistence, we made love again. I suffered no pain and began to enjoy it. After some time, my fluids seeped out and I felt a glow of tingling heat in my vagina. It was a very strange pleasure, and one that I had never before experienced.

"What a wonderful feeling!" I exclaimed. "This is probably the exact excitement the young woman told me about."

In the next ten days or so, we made love over and over, and I reached the point that I could accept him without feeling any pain at all. Every day before evening descended, I would think of sexual coupling and would urge Huimin to do it with me when we were in bed at night.

Out of curiosity, I once looked at my vulva, only to find that it did not look like a bud about to burst any more. Instead, it was now loose enough to contain a finger!

On one occasion, I woke up in the dead of night. Huimin, feeling amorous, engaged me in intercourse. We were just in the midst of our activities when my sister suddenly rose to use the bathroom, and the creaking of the bed gave rise to suspicion on her part. Sliding her hand under my quilt, she found that Huimin and I were spooned closely against each other, our thighs entwined.

"Why are you sleeping in such a manner?" she asked with a smirk.

I signalled to Huimin that he should groan, and then said to my sister, "He is having a stomach-ache. It was not enough to rub his belly or to wrap him up with my quilt. He has caught cold, so I had to warm him up by joining our bodies together. He is getting much better now."

"A fine doctor you are!" said my sister.

Presently she drifted off again. I was feeling an itch, and nudged Huimin to continue. Emboldened by my encouragement, he started pumping furiously, so much so that the bed shook and the hooks of the bed curtains rattled. The sounds awakened my sister.

"How vexing you are," she grumbled. "You allow me no peace to sleep!"

I was frightened, and had to end our intercourse.

The next day, my sister complained about us to Mother, telling her how we had disturbed her during the night.

"Huimin shared the bed with us," she reported, "and with three persons crammed in together I couldn't sleep well."

Mother was startled.

"Who allowed him to share the bed with you?" she asked.

"Elder Sister," said my younger sister. "Huimin kept begging her, and she found it hard to refuse him."

Mother spoke to Father in private: "Huimin is growing up, and it seems very likely that he is having indecent thoughts. Besides, Enuo is the same age as he, and has already reached the age of puberty. I think it best that he be moved outside to sleep."

"Agreed," said my father.

Before long, Huimin's nightclothes were removed from our bed. I lamented his dismissal, knowing that it must have been my sister who had betrayed us. In spite of my vexation with her, on the surface at least, I remained as friendly to her as ever.

Now that Huimin was no longer sleeping with us, I could see him only during the day. However, some clever maids, who had probably been prejudiced by my sister's words, kept a constant watch on me, making it nearly impossible for me to approach him. Filled with bitter resentment, I copied a poem onto a scroll in the regular style of calligraphy, intending to give it to him. The poem ran:

For Huimin:
My pillow square, so exquisite!
So too, my embroidered bed!
Alas, without my paramour,
No sleep till sun is red.[21]

Putting the scroll inside my sleeve I went looking for Huimin, but he had already returned to his parents' home. Each time I yearned for him at night I could hardly sleep a wink. My pillowcase was soaked with my tears, and my undergarments, with my secretions.

By the age of fourteen or fifteen I had grown into a stunning beauty. My sister had also become more attractive, and was prettier than ever. We often competed with each other, decking ourselves out with the new dresses we received.

"I am Feiyan," I said, "and you are Hede."[22]

"Then, whom are you missing more, Bird Killer or Red Phoenix?"[23] my sister taunted me.

---

21 This is the third stanza of the poem "*Gesheng*" in the *Tang* section of *The Book of Poetry*.

22 The allusion is to the tale "*Feiyan waizhuan*" (The Unofficial Biography of Zhao Feiyan). The tale recounts how Feiyan and her younger sister Hede were chosen by Emperor Cheng of the Han dynasty as his concubines, and how Feiyan later became his Empress, while Hede remained in his harem and continued to enjoy his favor.

23 Before entering the palace, Feiyan had a lover called "Sheniao" (Bird Killer). After she became Empress, she also established a secret liaison with a slave of the palace by the nickname of "Chifeng" (Red Phoenix). For details, see "The Unofficial Biography of Zhao Feiyan".

I covered her mouth with my hand, saying, "Later on, when you present the aphrodisiacs in Brocade Tent Seven, be sure that you feel no guilt because of your impetuosity!"[24]

My sister and I continued to live together for another three years until I reached the age of seventeen or eighteen. Even then, I could not forget my experience of sleeping with Huimin and the great tingling delight he had given me.

An old household slave of our family had a son whose name was Jun. Jun was seventeen or eighteen years of age, and being both handsome and a skilled musician, enjoyed great favor from my father, as his catamite.

"Perhaps," I thought, "this young man can provide me with what I wish I could still get from my cousin."

One time, I saw Jun passing by the window of my bedroom. I beckoned to him, teasing him in a provocative manner. Jun was wily. He first tickled my palm with his fingers several times and then snaked out his tongue.

"Why are you doing that?" I asked.

"Just take it into your mouth," he told me.

I did so. He then asked me to stick out my tongue the same way that he had done. As I snaked it out, he sucked it ravenously, which made me suddenly realize that this was what people called a "kiss." However, before we could proceed to more amorous games, someone approached and Jun immediately ran off. I then embroidered a scented wallet for him and in return, he gave me some cosmetic powder.

I began to lust after him.

When Jun indicated that he sought an assignation with me, I told him to meet me at dusk at the winding veranda. There I could avoid my sister who was with me almost all the time.

At the appointed hour, Jun was there. Thinking that he might thrill me as Huimin had done, I leaned against a pillar and removed my undergarments. Scarcely had I readied myself, however, when he launched his assault, and so violent was he, that it hurt me badly.

Terrified, I said, "You cannot assail me like this!"

Bestial and inconsiderate, Jun continued his fierce thrusts despite my protests. I could not endure the pain.

---

24 According to "The Unofficial Biography of Zhao Feiyan," it was in "Brocade Tent Nine" rather than in " Brocade Tent Seven" that Hede, royally drunk one night, fed Emperor Cheng, who was already very sick, seven *shenxiu* aphrodisiacs. According to the tale, he expired after an excessive number of ejaculations.

"Be gentle!" I exclaimed. "How can you make love with such a lack of consideration?"

"You have offered me this opportunity," he husked, "and now you want to back out!"

With these words, he launched another fierce assault, inflicting upon me such sharp pain that I could not help whimpering. Jun was cruel though, and continued his hard pounding.

"Please take pity!" I entreated.

He paid no heed, and rudely seized one of my legs, lifting it high.

"Jun!" I screamed, "Stop being so brutal!"

Hardly had I uttered these words than I heard voices approaching from a distance. Quickly I slipped into my underwear and made off with such speed that he was unable to stop me.

I had been badly hurt.

"What a terrible experience it was to toy with a tiger's whiskers!" I said to myself. "I swear I will never again venture out in search of pleasure."

That year I married into the household of Luan,[25] wedding the scion of a high-ranking official in the State of Jin.[26] The patriarch of the Luan household was named Rao, and he had three sons. The eldest one, who was called Keshe, was a student at the National Academy. The second one, my husband, was called Keyong, and was a licentiate tutoring students at home. The youngest was called Ketao, and he was studying martial arts at a military academy.

Since I was not a stranger to sex, and had lain first with Huimin and then with Jun, I had a guilty conscience, fearing that my husband might be suspicious of my virtue. The first time he mounted me, he seemed to have little difficulty in the entry. Though I felt some slight pain, I pretended to groan as if I were hurting terribly, and tossed and twisted my body in feigned agony.

My husband took it for granted that I was a virgin.

"What a beautiful and virtuous wife I have married!" he praised. "What an ideal bride both for me and for my family!"[27]

---

25 "*Luan*" (surname) and "*luan*" (penis) are homophonous.

26 Jin, one of the contending states in the Warring States period was located principally in Shanxi, but part of it was in the southern sector of the Ming province of Hebei. This adds to our argument that the author and the protagonist of the tale are one and the same.

27 In the original Chinese text, Keyong's words consist of two lines from two different poems in *The Book of Poetry*. There are several other places in the text in which the author uses a phrase or a line from The *Book of Poetry*, but since they do not contain allusions, we have not footnoted them. It is clear that author, like the protagonist, was very familiar with this work.

Hearing this compliment, I blushed a deep red.

I did my best to wait attendance upon my Mother-in-law, and at no time did I dare to be inattentive to her wishes. Adulations were heaped upon me from all the other members of the family.

After living with me for a year or so, my husband went to another prefecture to pursue his studies. Since I was left alone at home with no one to keep me company, I was arranged to eat my meals with Sha, my sister-in-law. It was, however, tedious and unpleasant being with her.

Sha's husband, Keshe, had a household slave called Yinglang, who was twenty-one or twenty-two years old, fair-skinned and as handsome as a re-incarnation of Feng Zidu[28] of the Qin Palace. Since he served his master with his "rear courtyard,"[29] he wore no cap, though his hair had been dressed into the shape of a topknot. I often lusted after him with my eyes.

"He may be just the right man to provide me with the pleasures I seek," I mused.

On one occasion, I spied Yinglang at a time when there happened to be no one else around. I called out to him, but being shy, he was reluctant to approach me. I then bade my maid, Pink Peach, to invite him inside.

"The Second Junior Mistress asked me to give you her regards," the maid said to him. "Just a moment ago, she admired you and summoned you to come to her, but you did not even respond. She is annoyed. You should go and apologize to her."

"It is my good fortune to enjoy the good graces of the Junior Mistress," he said. "But I fear that since her boudoir is forbidden to outsiders, I dare not be the first to violate the rule against entering it. By so-doing, I would bring calamity upon myself."

"The Junior Mistress simply pities you. You are an underprivileged orphan, and she wishes to offer you food and clothing," said Pink Peach. "You should not stubbornly reject her kindness."

"It is the Mistress who has summoned me," he finally agreed, "so she is to blame if it is inappropriate. If I refuse to go when summoned, then I shall be held responsible for the consequences."

At length he decided to come.

I had just arisen from my afternoon nap, and was applying my make-up in front of my mirror. I was drowsy and languid with the warm spring weather

---

28 Feng Zidu was an historical figure legendary for his male beauty.

29 This, of course, is a euphemistic expression indicating that he was the passive partner in anal sex with his master, who seems to have denied him the capping ceremony by which a boy was recognized as a man. After the capping ceremony, sexual relations between man and boy were to cease.

and the fragrance of flowers. When Yinglang arrived, I was coy at first, but soon reached out my hand to his.

"What a coward you are!" I said playfully. "I have twice extended an invitation to you, and still you seem so very reluctant to pay me a visit!"

"Madam," he said, "you are a rare flower blooming in the garden. How can I, a lowly insect, do it some injury? I have never dared to imagine that as an insignificant slave, I could so closely approach such a grand lady without risking my very life. Now that you have commanded me, I am left with no option but to oblige you."

I led him, entwining my arm with his, into my bed. His body, after I had undressed him, was revealed to me in all its alabaster whiteness. I embraced him and drew his tongue into my mouth until I felt my passion aroused. I then parted my thighs to show him my charms, and his penis became instantly erect. He inserted it into me, providing me with so much tingling pleasure that I involuntarily raised my body to meet him, my arms and legs all going limp. He leapt upon me and then energetically began to move in and out. Sadly, he was not very strong physically, nor did he have much sexual stamina. I had been in the state of enforced celibacy for so long that I was eager to take advantage of this opportunity to savor his delights, but before I was satisfied, he had spent himself. In spite of the fact that I was less than satisfied and was feeling some resentment, I could not but take pity on him.

"This was our first time and certainly it was not too bad," I said, placating him. "My boudoir is empty and I often feel lonely. When the days drag on and on with little change, how can I wile away my tedious hours without your company?"

I bade him come to me every night. We carried on in this fashion for several months, indulging ourselves in every variety of erotic pleasure. My body seemed to exist only for him, and he, too, seemed ready to die for me if necessary.

One day, when the maids were away, I was strolling along in the garden by myself. I was plucking blossoms to decorate my hairpins when I accidentally encountered Yinglang amidst the flowers. He desired to engage me in coitus right then and there, but I refused.

"No," I said, "someone might happen along."

"So what?" he said. "I don't care!"

For fear that my refusal might offend him, I allowed him to coerce me into removing my undergarments, and standing upright, permitted him to have his way with me. Forcefully, he thrust himself inside, and after no more than a hundred strokes, his sperm gushed forth like a fountain. He then pressed his body tightly against mine and fell silent, incapable of uttering a single word for a long while.

After some time, he gasped, "Ah, what fantastic pleasure! I was almost dying from it!"

Having been on my feet for so long I found my two legs exhausted and limp, and my loins weak and fatigued. We then sat down clasping each other.

Suddenly, another slave named Datu came upon us. Since I had not treated him well in the past, I was at a loss as to how to deal with the situation. To make the things worse, Datu had caught sight of my undergarments spread out on the ground. He was a boorish sort of a fellow, and was shocked to see us together.

"How dare you do such a thing here!" he shouted. "Yinglang! Are you courting death? If I conceal what I have seen today, how do you think I could face my master without shame?"

I felt terribly guilty and was filled with regret.

"I beg you to say nothing," I implored.

"Since it has already happened," said Yinglang, "I can only appeal to your generosity, hoping for mercy. I would be willing to let you share the favors of the Junior Mistress if that is what it would take."

Datu guffawed.

"Is that your way of keeping my mouth shut?" he asked. "Fine, then. I will keep my lips tightly sealed!"

He immediately made clear his intention to ravish me, and I could not refuse, since it was I who had brought this disaster upon myself. I directed Yinglang to carry me over onto his lap, and as he did so, he used his skill at anal sex to stealthily apply some spittle to his penis and work his way into my "rear courtyard." At the same time, Datu mounted his frontal assault, wild and unrestrained. True, his endowment was much larger and more formidable than that of Yinglang, but since he lacked Yinglang's warmth and romance, his copulation with me was harsh and jarring and I felt hardly any enjoyment. I felt only that my insides had been painfully plundered.

Datu then held my cheeks in his hands, snickering.

"Had I not caught you in adultery," he jibed, "how would it have been possible that you would permit me such liberties?"

"How dare you ridicule me," I retorted, "while you are savoring the charms of my body?"

Having tried out all his limited erotic skills, Datu then attempted to kiss me on the lips. I could not bear his garlicky, alcoholic breath and covered my mouth with my sleeve, but he yanked it away. I then turned my face toward Yinglang, but using both of his hands, Datu wrenched it back, and seemed determined to kiss me on the mouth. When I turned my head to the left he turned left, and when I turned it to the right he turned right. Finally, after quite some while, a cough in the distance liberated me from his clutches. As he removed his hands, I swiftly donned my clothes and took flight.

In my hurry to escape, I was forced to carry my undergarments since I had not had time to fasten the ties, and to my misfortune, I encountered my brother-in-law in the central section of the Winding Veranda. This was none other than Keshe, and he was astonished to see me in so awkward a panic.

"Why is Sister-in-law in such a hurry?" he inquired.

I was too ashamed to answer.

Suddenly, by accident, my undergarments slipped from my hands and fell to the ground. Elder Brother-in-law burst out laughing.

"Aha," he said, "Sister-in-law must have been having a tryst?"

I made no reply, wishing only to be rid of him as quickly as possible.

Elder Brother-in-law stepped forward and picked up my underwear.

"Be nice to me," he said. "If you refuse, I shall tell my brother!"

"If you tell my husband, I shall tell your wife!" I threatened.

Elder Brother-in-law laughed.

"What can you tell my wife?" he asked.

"I shall tell her that you attempted to rape me," I said.

"But I have done nothing," he said. "If we do have a little fun with each other, you can tell her whatever you like."

I laughed, and Elder Brother-in-law chuckled too. As I stood up, he promptly approached me from behind, lifted my dress, and then laying hold of my hips, crushed himself against me. I bent over a little to receive him. He then started to thrust himself between my thighs, where there still remained some semen from Yinglang and Datu.

Suddenly, looking at his palms, he blurted out, "Whose spittle has soiled my hands?"

He wiped his hands on my pants.

"Don't stain them!" I yelped at him.

"What is the point of being so fussy about your pants," he said, "when you have already had your body defiled?"

"Elder Brother-in-law, how can you be so inhuman as to ridicule me while you try to have sex with me?" I exclaimed.

I shoved him hard, and knocked him over. As I was about to take flight, I became aware that he was still holding fast to the ties of my underclothes.

Getting up, he apologized to me.

"Pray forgive my inappropriate words," he said, kneeling on the ground.

I had no intention of compromising.

Pretending to be angry, he tore free the ties from my underclothes. "So you won't comply?" he asked.

"No, I won't," I said.

He then began to walk away, taking the ties with him.

"Well, this is the evidence," he said. "I shall tell the whole world about your scandalous behavior!"

"Come back!" I shouted, frantically beckoning to him.

Hearing me call, he returned immediately, quite triumphant. Coerced though I was into intercourse with him, I found that his endowment, instead of being the size of Yinglang's as I had imagined, was even larger than that of Datu! Of course I could not receive it comfortably.

"Could you kindly not go so deeply?" I said hastily, trying to stop him.

He was, however, inflamed with passion and kept ramming his penis furiously into me, ignoring my pleas. Suddenly, I felt a stab of great pleasure mixed with the pain. I realized then that pain was perhaps inevitable for heightened enjoyment, and therefore permitted him to thrust as hard as he wished until he exploded. He then released me, his object both wilted and as soft as cotton floss, incapable of disporting itself again.

Only after that was I able to return to my bedroom.

"Although I have not yet finished narrating my story," said Shangguan to Qiongke, "it is now becoming late. Please allow me to return tomorrow to continue."

Qiongke agreed, and she took her leave.

Part II

The next day, Shangguan returned.

She said, "since I did not finish my story yesterday, I would like to continue today."

Even now, as I recall how I was first raped by Datu, and then forced into sex with Keshe, I still brim with resentment. My husband, who divided his time between home and his business outside, was at that time more frequently away than at home. Keshe, engaged in his father's business, was also seldom at home.

His wife, Sha, was a woman of some appeal. I observed her in private and found that she did not engage in any clandestine affairs, but when Keshe was away, she would sometimes sigh or moan midst the flowers in the morning, or beneath the moon at night, and would sometimes forget to eat or neglect her sleep.

The reason was simple.

Father-in-law, Master Luan, whose wife's health was very poor, was attempting to establish a sexual liaison with her.

One day, early in the morning, Sha was washing her face and applying her makeup when Father-in-law crept up behind her on tiptoe. He seized her hands, startling her greatly. Sha was about to scream when she saw that it was Father-in-law, and embarrassed, she stifled her shriek. Father in-law then eagerly fondled her breasts.

"Why are you doing this to me?" Sha squealed, as she splashed water from her basin onto his face.

Father-in-law responded at once by reciting the couplet Empress Wu had improvised for Emperor Gaozong:

How fortunate that before even in the brocade tent we meet,
I have sprinkles of dew from your golden basin received.[30]

(Madam Hibiscus comments: "Splashing his face with water indicates that she was already showing interest. Why is she now striking such a pose of innocence?!")[31]

Exerting all his strength, Father-in-law lifted Sha onto the bed. Although she struggled to free herself, she was unsuccessful since her maid, who might have helped her, happened to be absent at the time.

Angered and exasperated, she cried out.

"Father! Why are you doing this to me?"

Before she could finish speaking, however, Father-in-law had already dropped to his knees. "Save my life!" he exclaimed, and in the meantime, ran his hands under her dress to grope her private parts.

"I shall tell Mother-in-law," she threatened.

"It was I who permitted you to marry into my family," he rejoined, "and I have the right to enjoy your favors! Even if you do tattle to your Mother-in-law, what can she do about it?"

---

30 These two lines are quoted from *Lord of Perfect Satisfaction*, suggesting that Madame Hibiscus was familiar with the earlier work.

31 In the edition published in Qing dynasty, upon which this translation is based, there are many interlinear comments. All are anonymous, and in most cases, irrelevant to the translation. We include this one because it seems certain that it was made by the author herself, and indicates not only her gender, but since we believe that Enuo is her *alter ego*, it shows her genuine dislike for her sister-in-law whom she has already described as rather disagreeable.

He raised her legs and locked them around his waist, while he brushed his beard against her cheeks and neck. After a while she grew silent, letting him make free with her body.

It so happened that at the time, I was on my way to ask my sister-in-law about a personal matter, and entering her private quarters inquired about her whereabouts from her maid.

"In the bedroom," the maid answered.

When I entered, I saw that the bed curtains had been lowered. The bed was shaking and creaking, the curtains fluttering and the curtain-hooks rattling. I giggled.

"Sister-in-law," I called, "are you dreaming? Are you dreaming that your husband has returned home?"

As I pushed the bed curtains aside I saw that Father-in-law was on top of her, both of them naked. I broke into laughter. Father-in-law reached out at once and caught hold of my blouse before I could retreat.

"Seize her so that she cannot betray us!" Sha cried.

"Don't be preposterous!" I protested. "Sister-in-law, you are not only doing something vile but are also attempting to implicate me. What makes you think that I am like you?"

Father-in-law leapt gingerly from the bed. Wrapping his arms about me, he began to grind his penis against my body. Recalling the rumors I had heard about incestuous behavior by the fathers-in-law of others, I scoffed to myself, covering my face with my sleeve. I realized then that such things could indeed occur in the real world.

I refused to submit to his violation and was resisting as much as possible when Sister-in-law came to his aid. Reaching out from the bed she seized my arms and dragged me forcibly onto it with her. In the end, as I lay there, Father-in-law succeeded in throwing my legs high.

"Father," I screamed, "you are raping me and Sister-in-law is helping you! Both of you are behaving like animals!"

Then I could utter no more protests since Father-in-law pressed his beard against my lips.

"Father-in-law is our closest kin," said Sha with such an excuse. "Today we are serving him with our bodies. Should this not be considered filial conduct?"

I could not suppress a rueful laugh.

"I have never heard that a grotto penetrated by a son could also be penetrated by his father," I said. "What if the woman becomes pregnant after intercourse with both? Will the child be a son or a grandson?"

Father-in-law laughed with irony.

"You are both my beautiful wives," he said. "So pray be not too concerned about your dying Mother-in-law and your profligate husbands."

Seeing that Sha had abandoned any pretense to chastity, I was no longer able to hold myself back. I slurped Father-in-law's tongue into my mouth. It was flat and large rather than lean and pointed and filled my mouth to such an extent that I felt I was hardly able to suck it. I found, though, that Father-in-law's endowment, in comparison with those of Datu and Yinglang, was only mediocre, about the same size as my husband's.

Father-in-law plunged first into me, and then into Sha.

Since this was the first time he had seduced either of us, he was careful not to linger too long on one or the other, lest if one were neglected, she might change her mind. Thus he would grasp Sha while coupling with me, and caress me while lunging into her. Suddenly I felt a surge of arousal, and sought the pleasure he could stir up with his frenzied thrusts into me. I was frustrated, however, whenever he was reluctant to switch his attentions from Sha to me. After he had alternated with us for quite some time, I saw that he was on the verge of eruption. Squeezing him tightly, I refused to relinquish him, despite his impotent efforts to transfer his spew to Sha. Imprisoning him in my grip, I succeeded in compelling him to discharge inside me, and the reception of his fluid saturated me with great satisfaction.

Father-in-law, after all, was a middle-aged man; and after ejaculating in me, he was no longer able to make love to Sha.

When Father-in-law was burying his shaft into her, Sha splayed out her legs and encircled his neck with her arms; when he engaged in congress with me, I gyrated my hips and snaked out my tongue. Since all of our lewd and wanton techniques had been on full display, we could not but restrain ourselves from teasing each other. What left me unsatisfied was that Father-in-law's vigor and vitality were fading and his member, though capable of achieving full erection, was not sufficiently stiff, lacking the strength to "topple the mountains and overturn the seas."

"I am a normal woman," I said to Sha. "Since my husband is so often away from home and I have been living by myself for years, I really need a lover to fulfill my needs. To have an intimate relationship with our household slaves is not impossible, but they are very untrustworthy and their bodies are filthy and odorous. To take strangers from outside these walls is another option, but they may make public our liaisons. I have learned that Mother-in-law is on so much medication that she is no longer able to indulge Father-in-law in his erotic pleasures. Since we are both young and attractive, perhaps we should take turns to gratify him, and in this way, there will be no scandal outside the compound of our household. Is this not a happy plan?"

"I am concerned only that you might become jealous of me," said Sha.

"I promise that I shall not," I said.

"You may say that," she replied, "but just now, when Father-in-law was pounding away hard enough to both excite and satisfy us, you clasped him tightly, and refused to release him. This kind of thing might happen again and I would be able only to moisten my lips and never be able to drink my fill."

I was embarrassed, shamed by my actions.

"At that time, I was so aroused I could not help myself," I explained. "From now on, whenever Father-in-law achieves erection, I promise I will give way to you. Let us divide the days into odd and even numbers, and each of us will sleep with him on our designated dates."

One day I was in the midst of my bath when Father-in-law knocked on my door, disheveled and barefooted. My maid was at the time taking her own bath somewhere else and the door was left unlocked. Father-in-law pushed the door open and saw me emerging from the water.

"Ah, a lotus arises from the pond!" he exclaimed.

I dried myself hastily and leapt onto the bed. Father-in-law fell upon me. Our copulation satisfied me fully.

"Daddy," I flirted, "I am so thrilled that you came to see me. I am wondering now how you would compare me with Sha?"

"She is already thirty-years-old, and her channel is wide like a river," he replied. "How can she compare with you? Moreover, she is like a warrior holding a sharp spear as her waves of desire surge high. I fear that I cannot keep up with her. Besides that, you are much cleaner than she."

I was aware that my vagina lacked neither the "spear" nor the "surging waves" that he had described, and it was only because he loved me more that he uttered those honeyed words.

I carried on the affair with Father-in-law for several years. When my husband returned home, my Father-in-law dallied with Sha, and when Keshe returned, he slept with me. Our affair, in spite of being disrupted from time to time, never really ceased. It was not until much later when Father-in-law had become old and infirm and less interested in sexual amusements, that I began to feel discontented. I then resumed my relationship with Yinglang.

On one occasion, when Mother-in-law's medical condition worsened, I decided to seek a prognostication on her behalf.

Yinglang offered me advice, saying, "The Temple of Vacuity located at the western edge of the town is highly-regarded, and its deities are especially powerful. I suggest that you go there to obtain an oracle."

There I went the next day, in heavy make-up, with slaves of our household serving as sedan-carriers and Yinglang as my escort. After finishing my prayers,

I asked a monk of the temple whether the oracle boded ill or well for my mother-in-law's disease, but he made no reply.

This monk, whose name was Ruhai, had previously had a "rear-courtyard" relationship with Yinglang, and was so captivated by my beauty that he begged his erstwhile partner to arrange an assignation for himself with me.

"That should not be difficult," said Yinglang to him. "To have your wish fulfilled, you need only invite her to take lunch with you."

Ruhai was overjoyed. He came out and said to me, "The outcome of your divination was good. In ten days or so, your mother-in-law will be fully recovered from her illness."

Delighted, I was preparing to return home when he stopped me.

"Madam, pray remain for a vegetarian lunch," he said.

"I am afraid that the donation I have made to you is not sufficient for that," I said. "What a pity!"

Yinglang broke in. "We have travelled a long distance, and the sedan-bearers are all hungry. Now that this elder monk has invited you to lunch, why not just accept his kindness? You may pay him afterwards if you wish."

"I suppose so," I agreed, and was then led into the abbot's chamber.

"Junior Mistress," said Yinglang, "pray allow me to eat with the sedan-bearers in the kitchen while you are dining here."

He exited without even receiving my permission. Ruhai closed the door behind him.

Now that I was able to look more closely at the monk, I found him quite handsome. Though I was pleased, I nevertheless remained on my guard for fear that Yinglang might burst in, completely unaware that he had already betrayed me.

Ruhai, out of his mind with excitement, immediately threw his arms around me. He was so anxious to begin making love with me that I felt my arousal growing. "You wanted to give me something to eat," I said smiling, "but in fact it is I who am now feeding you!"

He unfastened my dress.

"You had better remove only my lower garments," I warned.

He undid the belt of my skirt, and together, we climbed onto the meditation bed.

Ruhai was a man of wide experience when it came to sodomizing acolytes, but who would have thought he had so little knowledge of the female anatomy!

He drove his penis into my "rear courtyard."

I realized then that this sort of intercourse was the favorite of men who loved men. Since I had, however, done it once before with Yinglang, and since this was my second time, I did not object, letting him plunge into me as he liked, though I surreptitiously chuckled. Before he entered my aperture, he had first applied some spittle; but he had no sooner buried the head of his shaft there than I felt that all the surrounding muscle being split open. It hurt me so much that I could not stifle my cries.

"Be quiet," said Ruhai. "The abbot is in the next room and might come in here should he hear a woman's voice."

I was in such agony that as he attempted deeper penetration, I was convulsed with the fear of even more pain, and in desperation, twisted my body so quickly as to dislodge his member from my anus. I then covered it with my hands, and when he pulled them away, swiftly covered it with my dress.

Ruhai became impatient.

"Are you a virgin?" he asked. "Why is this hurting you so much?"

I burst out laughing in spite of my distress.

"I am not a virgin, you fool," I snorted, "but you are a Buddhist monk who knows nothing of the Daoist way!"[32]

He was stunned.

"Is the woman's way different?" he asked.

"Get up and I will show you," I said.

Filled with suspicion, he was rather reluctant to rise, thinking that I might be tricking him so that I could escape. It was not until I guided his hand into my vagina that he knew that he had been very much mistaken. He then bent over to gaze at it, and in a state of extreme heat, kissed it repeatedly.

"How marvelous this treasure!" he exclaimed. "I have never seen anything like it!"

"This is the 'little Dharma gate'," [33] I told him. "It is especially designed for the entry and exit of a 'little monk'"[34]

Upon hearing this, he instantly lifted my legs, and locking them over his shoulders, rammed his 'little monk' straight into me. Since this was his first time having intercourse with a woman, he was too agitated to contain himself. It took him only a few thrusts before he erupted.

---

32 Buddhism and Daoism, after centuries of rivalry, had by the Ming come to stand as polar opposites, and here stand for the male and female genders. Daoism, from the beginning had valorized the female principle and in Chinese sexual manuals, it was usually a female like the "Woman Plain," who instructed men in the ways of intercourse. The meaning of this sentence is: "You are a man who knows nothing of the female sexual body."

33 A Buddhist metaphor for vagina.

34 A Buddhist metaphor for penis.

"Though my juices have spent," he muttered, "I do not yet feel satisfied. What should I do?"

"There is nothing I can do for your problem," I laughed. "Indeed, your 'little monk' seems to be one of those who are prone to intoxication before even entering the gate."

He was reluctant to part from me, and placed his member against my "gate" hoping that if he could restore his erection, he would be able to re-enter. His attempt, however, failed, and upon my insistence he had to release me. I dried my nether parts with a towel, while he did the same for himself.

I was about to depart when suddenly Ruhai's master leapt out from behind the bed and seized me, entreating me to lie down with him. I had no alternative but to let him have his way.

By that time I was very anxious to return home, and I reluctantly allowed him to reach his climax without even taking the time to inquire as to his Dharma name.

When I hastened out of the room, I saw no sign of Yinglang. I looked everywhere for him, and finally, inside the rear hall, found him amusing himself with some young acolytes.

I could not criticize him.

The youngest son of the Luan family, Ketao by name, had by this time, become quite familiar with the realm of sex; and though he had reached the age of twenty, was still unmarried. He seemed to have somehow learned of my dubious relations with Yinglang, and began to take every possible opportunity to pry into my private affairs. Cautious as I was in my dealings with him, he proved to be even craftier than I.

"Father works hard," he said to me one day. "With an abacus in hand he buries himself in his calculations, comparing prices over and over, and reckoning how much interest he can make from the capital he has invested. His industry enables us three sons to live a comfortable life. However, since Mother has been bedridden and there are no attractive maids around, I really cannot fathom how he has been able to find someone with whom to enjoy himself."

Thinking that he must have discovered our secret liaisons, I sprang to my own defense. "What I did, I did with with Sha's co-operation," I said with a smile in my voice. "Why should Younger Brother-in-law direct his scorn only at me?"

Actually, Ketao had not been certain that intimate relations had taken place between myself and Father-in-law, but when he understood my meaning, he laughed aloud.

"Since you could do those things with Father-in-law in the presence of someone else," he said, "you can surely do them again with your Younger Brother-in-law when there is no one else around!"

I felt such shame that a pinkish glow suffused my cheeks.

"At that time your Elder Brother was not at home," I said. "But he is at home now, so your hope is in vain!"

"Today he is not in the house," said Ketao. "Let me do it with you immediately, or I shall tell him not only of your illicit relationship with Father-in-law but also of your trysts with Yinglang."

I dissolved into nervous laughter.

"To tell the truth," I said, "you caught my attention long ago. I have held myself back simply because I thought you might be unable to satisfy me. Why should I have wasted my time in futile pursuit with no certainty of reward? Now that you have come to me of your own volition, I suppose I have no reason to be fastidious."

Together, we climbed into the bed. I had imagined that Younger Brother-in-law's endowment, if not so large as that of Datu, would at least be the size of Father-in-law's. Who would have thought that it turned out to be even smaller than that of Yinglang! I could not help but burst out laughing.

Ketao had always claimed to be sexually experienced, and was oblivious to the fact that I was mocking his prowess. He arched himself against my belly, thrusting over and over to the left and then to the right. But tiny as a grain of millet, his member was in no way able to stir up waves of any size in my enormous granary.

Suddenly he said, "Let me rest awhile."

I said nothing, but sneered at him in my mind. As a paramour, he had more than enough ardor but insufficient staying power. For me, he was a man incapable of arousing my strong sexual desires and worthy, therefore, only of scorn. Unaware, however, that there were others whose company I enjoyed far more than his, Ketao wallowed in his own self-satisfaction.

Before long I was pregnant.

"Whose child is this?" I pondered. "Does it belong to Yinglang? Datu? Elder Brother-in-law? Younger Brother-in-law? Father-in-law? My husband? Or one of those two monks?"

When the child was born, I was unable, even myself, to tell from his appearance who the father might be, since the child did not particularly resemble any of them. "Anyway," I thought, "one of them must be the father!"

My younger sister, Xianjuan, had married into a family called Fei. My brother-in-law, her husband, was also a licentiate making a living by tutoring students. He enjoyed a good relationship with my husband, and since they often spent time together discussing the meanings of various literary works, they soon became fast friends. As his sister-in-law, I often encountered him—a tall and sturdy man, with a large nose like a bottle.

"A large-nosed man must also have a big cock," I mused.

I decided to establish a more intimate acquaintance with him, and sent Yinglang to convey my intention. Fei was elated when he leaned of my desire, for he had always been very interested in me.

It so happened that one day my husband invited him for a drink. After quaffing several cups, my husband fell into a drunken stupor. He bade Fei to rest awhile in his study while he himself went into the bedroom to sleep.

Soon my husband was in a sound slumber, snoring thunderously. Quietly, I slipped out of our room to see Fei, who was happily astonished. Not saying a word, he took me onto his lap and positioned me with my face toward him. I found, as he thrust into me, that his member was only of medium size, not as large as I had expected. I felt I had been hoodwinked: a man with a big nose does not necessarily have a big penis as so many people claim! Despite its size, his erection was extremely hard and was hot like fire, so it gave me great pleasure. Sitting upright, he held my waist and bounced me up and down while he remained absolutely still. Following his tempo as he hefted me up and shoved me down, I began to gyrate my own body, producing in myself even greater stimulation.

"Brother-in-law," I gasped, "what a marvelous technique this is! I feel as if my soul were about to fly away."

He only smirked and made no reply. He turned me around, making me now sit on his lap with my back toward him. After entering me from behind he once again bounced me up and down as he had done before, and I squirmed in time with his rhythm. I was drowning with pleasure.

"This is just too fantastic!" I panted.

Fei, however, was unable to hold out for long, and all too soon, he came. I had still not had enough, and was unwilling to rise. He then hefted me up and down once more until I was spasming, experiencing such sensations that it felt that my skin was being stung by a host of mosquitoes and my ears were being brushed by a whisk. I was totally satiated.

"I have now obtained one more lover!" I mused.

Yinglang's voice broke in upon my thoughts.

"Mistress," he called, "please wake up."

I said to Fei, "I will release you after you come one more time."

He asked me then to stand up and bend a little over the chair in front of me, so that he could rise to his feet and lunge into me from behind without lifting me up and down. This time he was violent, like a warrior with a weapon in hand and his armor buckled on. I bent over, aflame with lust, to observe the manner of our coupling. Before long, my grotto was once again flooded. With his cannon mounted deep within me, I could only imagine how far the shells would fly! In spite of having spent twice, he remained as virile and vigorous as ever. At last, his instrument, still lodged inside my orifice, began to lose its previous heat and hardness.

"You must be exhausted," I said.

I rose, and then went on to say with a smile, "You already have a wife of your own, and now you have reached out your hand to your wife's elder sister! Your appetites must be hard to satisfy. As for me, the pleasure and the ecstasy I have received both on your lap and bent over the chair, have brought me complete satisfaction. I think I must now take my leave."

He did not try to detain me.

When I was about to re-enter my bedroom, Yinglang came up behind me, and said in a low voice, "Mistress, would you allow me also to partake of your charms? I have been watching your activities for so long that I am bursting for release."

"As you wish," I said. "I suppose I ought to show my gratitude for your service as my go-between."

Standing right there, we united our bodies; but Yinglang came quickly, before I could even feel his strokes.

It was for this reason that I sought him out for sex only on rare occasions. Most of the time, there was no guarantee at all that he could provide me with the gratification I desired.

Father-in-law's birthday was in early autumn. Prior to that day he came to me, not to Sha, for amorous amusement.

"Happy birthday to you!" I said.

On his birthday, his three sons held a dinner party for him. There were four tables of guests, and actors were engaged to perform a play in the courtyard. The cast included both stock male characters like an official, a soothsayer, and a jester, as well as stock female characters. The play performed was a Yuan drama, and I watched it from behind a screen. Among the actors playing the female roles was a youth called Xiangchan, who was, I noticed, extremely graceful, elegant, and charming. No wonder he was a favorite of the wealthy patrons of theatre! I observed him closely. His costume was diaphanous and light and his forehead and eyes resembled those of a fine portrait. His beauty was comparable to that of a lady fair and his clear and melodious tones, lingering in the air and enticing even the clouds to stop to listen, were as exquisite as the music of a full orchestra. Finding him irresistible, I secretly dispatched a female slave to present him with a cup of tea.

"The Second Junior Mistress confers upon you a cup of green jade tea," the slave girl said.

Xiangchan sipped it and was delighted to discover that what made the tea so fragrant was not the addition of herbs as he had thought, but two gold rings, nine pearls, and an amber eardrop. He understood very well its significance. He finished the tea and put away the precious gifts, but he dared not to come to me immediately for fear that he might be seen by the audience scattered around.

In the middle of the banquet, my husband had received a visit from a friend and had been forced to leave the party. For reasons unknown to me, he had not yet returned when the play drew to its end. Once again, I surreptitiously dispatched the slave girl to Xiangchan.

"The Second Junior Mistress would like to invite you to call upon her and instruct her on how to write some characters," she said to him.

He demurred.

"I do not know how to write," he said, "so how can I teach her?"

"The Mistress orders you to come," the slave girl insisted. "Do not refuse her request."

"Since she has made this a command," he said, "I shall have to come without delay. But the pathway to her quarters is long and winding, and there are people all around, so it is very likely that I shall be observed by someone while I make my way through the crowds. Moreover, should I depart so suddenly, my fellow actors may become suspicious."

"Do not concern yourself with the winding pathways and the throngs," urged my maid. "I will be your guide and will shield you from inquisitive eyes. As long as I accompany you, any of your colleagues who might be suspicious will have no reason to question you."

Xiangchan then removed his female costume and donned his own clothes. What a beautiful young man he was! What an ideal husband for girls of marriageable age!

My clever slave-girl finally ushered him into my chamber.

I was not at all embarrassed that I had taken it upon myself to proffer the invitation. I was seated beneath a lamp, my face skillfully made-up. I bade the slave to close the door and then took him into my arms.

"What a handsome youth you are!" I said. "Are you Wang Zijin?[35] Are you Pan Anren?"[36]

---

[35] Wang Zijin, or Wang Ziqiao, was a legendary immortal in Chinese mythology, and an

"No, I am neither of them," he laughed. "I am a simple passerby who has happened into this great house. This is a meeting destined by Heaven. What more can I say? Tomorrow when I recollect today's events, I shall probably think it was a dream."

"If you do not rebuff me," I murmured, "how could I reject you, as if I were discarding some leftovers?" I lay back on the chair and raised my legs. Xiangchan wasted no time driving his cock into me. His organ, like that of most men, was by no means extraordinary, but it was certainly much larger than that of my brother-in-law, Ketao. Once it was inside me, however, it felt like a vibrating cymbal dangling in the middle of a large bell. I doubted that it could give me much pleasure.

I gazed at him under the light. His countenance appeared like crystal, mesmerizing me. I was infatuated and gazed upon his face for a long while.

"Your beauty is a feast for my eyes," I said, "and I consider myself far too ugly to be your equal. The only reason I insisted that we make love was my sincere hope that we not forget each other when it is all over. Shall we ever meet again? I do not know, but I know that I shall pine for you. How tragic! How very sad!"

"Madam," said Xiangchan, "I feel mortified that I do not possess an organ of sufficient size to fully gratify you. You were kind enough to insist that I visit you, and I have made a fool of myself with my incompetence. Still, you did not reproach me. How could I ever forget your fond affection?"

"If you love me and will not forget me, I shall have no regrets," I said.

I gave him an emerald hairpin as a souvenir.

Time sped by and before I knew it, it was several years later. During that whole period, I had not met one single interesting man, and had had to content myself with two or three of my old sexual partners, who slept with me in turn as they had done before.

The son I had borne some years ago, Shengwu, had now reached school age. I considered sending him to a private school in the countryside but was afraid that there might be too many children there and that he might spend too much time playing with them. Finally I decided to engage a tutor, a scholar from Zhaoge county,[37] whose surname was Gu, and whose given name was Deyin. He was thirty-years-old, masculine and robust. He was both serious and careful in supervising my son's studies.

---

archetype of male beauty.

36 Pan Anren, or Pan Yue (247–300), was a famous poet in the Jin dynasty. He is said to have been very handsome.

37 Zhaoge county is in the northern part of present-day Henan province.

I cooked meals for him every day, in an attempt to show that I was very well disposed toward him. My ultimate goal was to seduce him, but for fear of his possible indiscretion, I hesitated to approach him directly.

That year my husband took a position in a distant location. I was now well over thirty, and though my beauty was beginning to fade, by the judicious use of make-up, I could still compare favorably to girls in their teens. As a woman in her thirties, however, my lust seemed to have grown stronger than ever, and it was agony for me to retire each night to my empty bed.

Before long, Ketao married and I moved my residence to the West House. Gu, who continued to teach my son, was lodged in the East House. The windows of the two buildings were far apart but facing each other, and when I was applying my makeup in the morning I often noticed Gu peering at me. In summertime, he frequently saw me disrobe entirely or simply bare my bosom. As he tutored my son, he usually sat by the window and would fix his eyes upon me whenever I was embroidering in front of my window.

"This clever teacher is aiming to seduce me," I thought. "How should I handle the situation?"

I was left at this time with only a single errand-boy, a lad by the name of Lingcui. He was young and dull, but had never refused to carry out any task I assigned him. I dispatched him to convey my greetings to the teacher.

Gu said to the boy, "Tell Junior Mistress that I am aware of her intentions and am very receptive to them. However, in view of the fact that her maids are all meddlesome and shrewish, I do not dare to approach her quarters and disturb her rest."

Lingcui returned and reported his words to me.

"Hmm," I mused to myself, "this man is very discreet! Perhaps I shall first send a slave-girl to test him. My senior maid, Green Lotus, is quite voluptuous and would be the ideal bait."

I summoned Green Lotus.

"Go to the East House and tell my son to return here for dinner," I said.

And away went Green Lotus. Gu seemed astute enough to understand my plan, and passionately forced himself on the maid for intercourse. Though at the beginning, Green Lotus resisted his impetuous advances, she soon surrendered and opened herself joyfully to him. Gu exerted every effort to please her, and succeeded in giving her complete satisfaction.

He then said, "I would like to sleep with your Junior Mistress."

"You must be patient," she replied. "I will help you when the opportunity presents itself."

Upon her return, Green Lotus reported to me in a persuasive and suggestive manner, "Master Gu is a very *manly* scholar!"

"Ah!" I said laughing, "you have had sex with him, haven't you? Perhaps we can share the fun!"

The maid was excited.

"I have reason to believe, Madam, that he is looking for that very thing," she confided to me. "Why not arrange a time with him?"

"How is his endowment?" I asked.

"Oh, extraordinarily large, like a donkey's, and robust," she replied.

"Perfect!" I said. "Tell him to come tonight."

When the moon was rising, Gu crept into the West House, and after ascending the stairs, bowed to me and said, "I deserve death for intruding into the women's quarters and offending the dignity of Your Ladyship."

"The breeze is so gentle and the moon is so bright," I said, in a husky voice. "How can I spend the night alone in my solitude. I have offered you this invitation so that we might converse and enjoy this beautiful evening together. There is no need to be so polite."

We sat down side by side. Feeling a surge of arousal I was no longer able to control myself.

"Perhaps it is time now for sleep," Green Lotus suggested.

We then disrobed, and snuffing out the candles, climbed into bed.

"You are so considerate to me and your blessings are boundless," whispered Gu. "Though I am but a mediocre steed, I shall nonetheless attempt to provide my rider with as much pleasure as I can."

He thrust himself into me. His member, quite unlike most of those I had previously experienced, was much larger than I could comfortably receive. As it made its way in, it swelled and flexed to fill my passage entirely, and voluptuous pleasure washed all over my body. As it was inserted completely into me, not a single inch of my passage was left unfilled, and every surface, on all sides, was fully and solidly occupied.

"Sir, how extraordinary your object is!" I exclaimed. "Had it not been for the recommendation of Green Lotus I would never have experienced such rapture! I imagine that not even the endowments of Lu Buwei[38] and Lao Du [39] were so massive!"

---

[38] Lu Buwei (?–235 BC) was the prime minister and reputedly, the biological father of the ruler of the State of Qin, who was to become the first emperor of China in 221 B.C. Lu was also well-known as the compiler of *Lushi chunqiu* (The Annals of Lu Buwei), a rich and comprehensive compendium that records the great variety of the beliefs and customs of that time. No reference is made in the "Biography of Lu Wuwei", in Sima Qian's *Shiji* to the size of his endowment. Perhaps the fact that he fathered first emperor garnered him a reputation for potency.

[39] Lao Du (?–238 BC), whose phallus was not only very large but was sturdy enough to

Indeed, his penis was enormous both in length and girth. It could penetrate deeply enough to reach the source of my greatest joy, soaking my loins with perspiration. It could also jerk spasmodically, expanding and contracting, without the motion of his body. As it throbbed and pounded, it was as if a spear were being driven into my nether parts. Saturated with delight, I could scarcely believe how copiously my torrent of desire flowed and spurted forth like a raging river. The mouth on the head of his erection could open and close, and when it fastened upon the bud in the neck of my womb, all my bones seemed to melt. Once I fainted in orgasmic climax, but he kept plunging into me, and not until after more than a hundred strokes, did he pause to take a breath.

"I am expiring in your hands," I moaned.

"If you were to die," he rejoined, "I would return your kindness by taking my own life."

"I have never before fallen into such a state of rapture," I gasped. "When you withdrew, it seemed to suck out my insides, and when you drove into me, it was so forceful that I thought you were drilling a hole in my vagina."

"Your vase," he replied. "is as rare as the opportunity to become the teacher of your son. The crater is not deep but is capable of reception, not shallow, but can be filled. It is not the tightest to be sure, but when I plunge into it, I am made aware of its ability to clasp."

"You love me dearly indeed," I sighed.

That night Gu and I indulged ourselves in so much erotic sport that we did not sleep a wink. Although I was exhausted, I was well content.

Happy and satisfied, I no longer showered my delicate attentions upon my other lovers, but devoted myself entirely to Gu. His family was poor and the clothes he wore were made of coarse fabric, so I began to make clothing for him. The materials I used for both the exterior and the interior sides were bright and beautiful brocade.

He kept me company every night, though sometimes he was too fatigued to meet my sexual demands. Out of consideration for him I concocted a herbal medicine that could replenish his marrow and strengthen his virility. I also provide him with some aphrodisiacs, directing him to take one pill every morning and evening. Before he ate his breakfast, I would feed him with *longan* or *ginseng* juice.

---

balance a chariot wheel on it when it was erect, was a secret lover of the First Emperor's mother. After she heard of his unusual attributes, she had his beard removed and made him a high-ranking "eunuch" in her own palace. See the "Biography of Lu Buwei," in Sima Qian's *Shiji*. .

Shortly after our affair began, I asked Ketao to send to his home a bolt of green brocade and some white-gold ingots. I even sold my hairpins and jade earrings to provide him with better meals.

Gu became arrogant.

If his meal was even a little late, he would angrily throw his bowls or dishes on the floor refusing to eat, no matter that there was a table of delicious food in front of him. I had no way of placating him but to re-cook the entire meal. Once he was well-fed, however, he was more affectionate in his nightly love-making, and more vigorous. I began to give full rein to my wanton and lecherous inclinations, and no longer felt guilty or ashamed of any of them. Since Green Lotus always waited on us, Gu was obliged to spend some time with her as well, but since she had acted as my intermediary I had no cause for complaint.

With my whole mind focused on Gu I had become estranged from Yinglang. Infuriated, he took counsel with Datu.

"I swear to bring their affair to light!" he said.

A short time later Yinglang hurled curses at Gu from a safe distance, so loudly that Father-in-law heard his tirade of vituperation. Father-in-law came to me immediately for an explanation, but I did not answer him in a respectful way. He then forced me to perform the act of love with him, and I did it only passively and in a perfunctory fashion. Father-in-law therefore became rather suspicious of me and began to nurse a grudge against me.

It had not been too long since I had last slept with Ketao, but now I tried to keep my distance from him. When he came to me for our usual bawdy dalliance, I treated him indifferently, withholding my previous tenderness. He was, of course, very unhappy at this, and after learning that I was unusually intimate with Gu, resented me bitterly.

The neighbors in our lane became unruly as soon as they caught wind of my scandal. They chanted:

Shangguan Enuo
Lies with a man from Zhaoge.
How very notorious is her fornication!
Can a whetstone erase her bad reputation?

This they said without even knowing of all the other men with whom I had enjoyed illicit relations! I now tossed aside my remaining scruples and engaged in intercourse with Gu wherever possible. Once I was caught in the act by Father-in-law and Ketao.

"How dare you be so brazen!" Father-in-law bellowed at me.

The scandal soon spread. Not daring to go directly to my husband, Datu spoke to my son instead. "You mother has been sleeping with your teacher!" he told him. "If you do not dismiss your teacher, it means that you are willing to condone her behavior!"

My son had now grown up, and Datu's words incited his indignation.

Fei, the husband of my younger sister, came to my home one day with the intention of renewing our former intimate relationship. I bluntly rejected him.

"I am getting old," I said, "am no longer capable of serving you. It was foolish of me years ago not to confine myself to where I should have been, and most assuredly, I cannot repeat this mistake once again."

Filled with suspicion, Fei made inquiries about me from Ketao, who disclosed to him that I had obtained a new lover.

"That damned fellow is courting death!" Fei cursed, "and that woman is really beyond shameless!"

Needless to say, Fei, too, hated me.

It so happened that on that same day, my cousin Huimin came to visit me. Though he was now nearly forty years of age, he had just recently become a licentiate and the purpose of his visit was simply to pay his respects to me. There was nothing amatory involved. But Gu, whom Huimin encountered as he entered the middle hall, thought that he might be one of my partners in adultery.

"This man will carve off my enjoyment," he thought.

"You bastard!" he shouted at Huimin. "How dare you enter this compound claiming that you are her cousin! Get out right away, or I shall set the dogs on you!"

Huimin became angry.

"This is simply a courtesy call," he answered just as loudly. "What gives you the right to curse me for no reason? Who are you, you damned sour prick and stinking balls?!"

He withdrew, retreated, and bumping into Fei on his way back home, related to him the incident which had just occurred.

"Shame on Sister-in-law!" said Fei. "In these recent days she has simply gone too far! The fellow who insulted you is none other than Gu, her lover."

Fei then told Huimin all the gory details of the story.

"I must tell her husband," said Huimin.

Huimin went looking for Keyong and told him everything he knew.

My husband was aghast.

"I thank you for letting me know," he said.

Yet in his own mind he still had his doubts.

"Is the story true?" he asked my son.

"I am afraid so," my son answered.

My husband then asked Father-in-law, "Have you ever heard of this affair?"

"Quite a few times," he admitted.

He then asked Ketao, "And did you also see them together?"

"Oh, on many occasions," Ketao answered.

My husband sighed.

"My wife's adultery has been so notorious that people on the street sing of it, friends and relatives know of it, and my entire family laughs at me behind my back. I am the only person who was kept in the dark. How stupid I have been!"

In a fury, he summoned me.

"You bitch!" he screamed. "I wish I could kill both you and that bastard, Gu! I would take you both to court, but I am not hardhearted enough. Bring him here!"

Gu was dragged in. He was shoved hard and fell to the floor.

"I beg you to spare my life!" he implored tearfully.

My husband ordered everyone in the family to take turns flogging him. Father-in-law went first, and then the rest in turn, laid several strokes on him. He howled like an ass braying, as his skin was broken and his blood splashed out.

Ketao finally intervened on his behalf.

"It is Sister-in-law who should take the blame," he said. "He does not deserve such harsh punishment."

Gu was then dragged out.

Enraged, my husband now snatched hold of my hair and struck me wherever he could lay his fist. I was too ashamed to protest.

"You are not only lewd but contemptible," he roared. "Why do you not hang yourself, here and now!"

I wept, my tears coursing down my cheeks. "I am lewd indeed," I sniffled, "but I beg you to spare my life. I will be willing to accept any punishment you deem fit and I promise solemnly that I will correct my misconduct."

"Ha, ha," laughed my husband grimly. "You are willing to accept corporal punishment only because you fear death. What a conniver you are! If you wish to choose the least painful death, I shall permit you to commit suicide with a cup of poison wine."

Father-in-law intervened.

"My second son," he said, "it is your misfortune to have acquired a wife so lewd and unfaithful. But I would prefer that you send her back to her parents' home rather than put her to death. That seems excessively cruel!"

"But such a punishment is precisely what she wants," said my husband furiously. "I can't let her off so easily!"

"If you must kill my mother," said my son, "then I must also kill myself!"

I wept bitterly, saying, "When even a mother having seven sons lived a miserable life,[40] how can I expect a better fate?"

"Daughter-in-law has always attended upon me carefully and with diligence," said Mother-in-law. "Now that this thing has happened, you should return her to her home in a decent way."

"All right," came my husband's grudging reply.

The writ of divorce deprived me of my status both as Keyong's wife and Shengwu's mother, and decreed that I was to be sent back to my mother's home without delay.

I sighed with regret.

I bade farewell to my son and then took my leave, making my way back home all alone. By that time my father had passed away and my mother, who had no male heir, did not unduly blame me for my transgressions.

"You may stay with me for the time being," she said.

That year I was thirty-nine years old.

Since I was divorced by my husband, one and all in the neighborhood knew my story, and every time I ventured out or returned home, someone would point his or her finger at me, saying, "There is that corrupt woman of the Luan household."

Dejected and remorseful, I said to myself, "In the middle stage of my life, I went astray, and was rewarded with my just deserts! When I was a maiden I was influenced by a young woman's words and slept with Huimin, which violated the relationship between cousins. Afterwards I seduced the slave, Jun, reducing myself to the status of a servant. After I was married, I slept with Yinglang and then was forced into intercourse with Datu, lowering once more my status as a mistress. I entered into incestuous liaisons with Father-in-law as well as with Elder Brother-in-law, and that violated the relationship between in-laws. I was sexually intimate with Ketao, which also breached the relationship between in-laws. Copulation with Fei was another type of violation of the relationship between in-laws and by fornicating with an actor and two monks, I profaned my respected status as a lady. Taking Gu as my lover, in effect, equated me with my employee. Outside of my marriage, I have had sexual relationships with twelve men altogether. These evil deeds were

40 The allusion is to the poem entitled "Kaifeng" (Southern Wind) in the *Bei* section of the *The Book of Poetry*.

beyond pardon, and I deserved to be cast off by my husband and my son. Now, as I suffer a lonely and celibate life, who is there to blame but myself?"

I bit my finger until it bled.

"I will never again indulge in carnal pleasures!" I vowed.

At the suggestion of my mother, I began to worship the Triratna.[41] Every day I recited my rosary and adhered strictly to a vegetarian diet. I confessed my sins with head bowed down. "The sea of desire and the mountain of sex have been overwhelmed with the crimes I have committed," I repented, "and I seek only to find some fresh, clean water with which to cleanse my lecherous heart!"

By that time, my ex-husband and his family had severed all relationship with me, and so too, had Huimin and Fei, who had never come to visit me even once. It was only Ruhai who, after hearing that I had been divorced and had become a devout disciple of Buddha, dispatched a monk to pay me a visit. Unaware that the monk was his messenger, I went out to welcome him.

Seeing that I was alone, the monk introduced himself. "I am a monk from the Temple of Vacuity," he said. No sooner did I hear these words than I realized that he had been sent by Ruhai. Blushing red, I rushed back into the house and called my boy-servant to drive him away.

I have endured thirty years of this lonely life, and now I am seventy years old. I have freed myself from all my former attachments to this world, and was not affected even when I heard that my son had acquired a fine local reputation for himself.

As I recollect my past, I feel that I have lived in a dream. I am old and no longer have fear of being ridiculed. That is why I could rattle on and tell you everything. Are you bored?

Here are a few remarks made by Qiongke:

The young woman's instructions on sexual matters would have remained unknown to anyone else had the old woman not disclosed them. Her tale is intriguing simply because it is her own story she is relating. Is she not foolish, leaving us this account of her own life as a woman crazed by love?

Her body is on Mount Wu[42] *yet her mind soars up to the clouds,*
Is it that she has lustful roots of previous life, one may doubt?
Leaving readers with an erotic story, Enuo feels shameful,
Yet pretty women with romances are now more than a handful.

---

[41] Triratna, or the "Three Treasures (*sanbao*), refers to Buddha, Buddhist scriptures, and the Buddhist clergy. Here it stands for Buddhism generally.

[42] A legendary place famous for sexual encounters.

Critique[43]

Shangguan, who had illicit sexual liaisons with twelve men, ended up divorced when her relations with Gu Deyin came to light. It was her loving devotion to this one, single man that brought the jealousy of all the others upon her. Her husband, Keyong, was hardly aware of her many amours and knew only of her affair with Gu when he abandoned her. How foolish he was! The publication of her memoir is therefore useful to those who wish to keep discipline in their boudoirs and take strict precautions.

43 This critique appears in the Chinese text as the ending of the story. Judging from its different moral tone, however, it must have been added by a different person when the story was in private circulation in manuscript form. When the book was published in the eighteenth century, this comment was integrated into the text, which has misled not only general readers but also scholars of Ming-Qing fiction.

Glossary

This glossary covers important characters, historical personages, names of authors, names of places, book titles, and special terms in both the texts and the footnotes. It does not include those that are common or unimportant, nor the names of authors and book titles that appear in the Selected Bibliography.

ao 凹

Beijing wawa 北京娃娃
beili zhi xiong 北里之雄
Beimen 北门
Bi Gan 比干

Cairen 才人
Changsun Wuji 长孙无忌
Chengdi 成帝
Chifeng 赤凤
Chong'er 重耳
Chu Suiliang 褚遂良
chuwu 畜物

Daguan yuan 大观园
dao 道
Di Renjia 狄仁杰
Ding Ling 丁玲
Ding Lingwei 丁令威
Donggong 东宫
Dong-Xi Jin yanyi 东西晋演义
Dou 窦

Enuo 婀娜

Feiyan waizhuan 飞燕外传
feng 封
Feng Zidu 冯子都
Fuqiu Bao 浮丘伯
Furong zhuren 芙蓉主人

Fusheng liuji 浮生六记

Gaozong 高宗
Gesheng 葛生
Gu Deyin 谷德音
Guan guo si zhi ren yi 观过斯知仁矣
Guilin 桂林

Haose yidai nan 好色一代男
Haose yidai nu 好色一代女
Hede 合德
Hongmen 鸿门
houting 后庭
Huayang Sanren 华阳散人
Huimin 慧敏

Ihara Saikabu 井原西鹤

jishu 鸡树
jishu 几树
Jiajing 嘉靖
Jiaotong 狡童
jiaoxia 交狎
Jin 晋
Jin Xianggong 晋献公
Jingzhou 荆州

Keshe 克奢
Ketao 克饕
Keyong 克慵
Kaifeng 凯风

Kunyu qingzhuan 阃娱情传

Lanling Xiaoxiaosheng 兰陵笑笑生
Lao Du 嫪毐
Li Chunfeng 李淳风
Li Dan 李旦
Li Shimin 李世民
Li Zhe 李哲
Li Zhi 李治
Liji 骊姬
Lingnan 岭南
Liu Bang 刘邦
Liu Bosheng 柳伯生
lu 炉
Luling 庐陵
Lu Buwei 吕不韦
Luhou 吕后
Lushi chunqiu 吕氏春秋
luan 卵
luan 栾
Luoyang 洛阳

mianshou 面首
Manzhu 满族
Mang 氓
Meiniang 媚娘
Mudanting 牡丹亭
Mugua 木瓜

Nahai 南海
Niu Jinqing 牛晋卿

pahui 扒灰
Pan Anren 潘安仁
pin 牝
pinkou 牝口
pinwu 牝屋
pinzhong 牝中

Qianshang 褰裳
Qingchi fanzheng daoshi 情痴反正道士
Qingchizi 情痴子
Qingdian Zhuren 情颠主人
Qiuci 龟兹

rouju 肉具

sanbao 三宝

Sha 沙
Shafei nushi de riji 莎菲女士的日记
shan 禅
Shangguan 上官
Shangguan wan'er 上官婉儿
Shanghai baobei 上海宝贝
Shanglinyuan 上林苑
Sheniao 射鸟
Shen Fu 沈复
Shen Huaiqiu 沈怀璆
Shen Nanqiu 沈南璆
Shenzong 神宗
Shengli 圣历
shi 势
Shijing 诗经
Sima Xiangru 司马相如
Sunu jing 素女经
suanluan choudan 酸卵臭蛋
Sun Kaidi 孙楷第
Sunzi bingfa 孙子兵法

Taishan 泰山
Taizong 太宗
Tang Xianzu 汤显祖
Tiaolangyue 挑浪月
tu 凸

Wanli 万历
Wang Yifu 王夷甫
Wang Zijin 王子晋
Wenhuang 文皇
wenyan 文言
Wujing 五经
Wushan 巫山
Wu Qi 吴起
Wu Chengsi 武承嗣
Wu Sansi 武三思
Wu Shihuo 武士镬
Wu Yue 武约
Wu Zetian 武则天

Xiliang 西凉
Xiang Yu 项羽
Xiao Shufei 萧淑妃
xiao yangchun 小阳春
Xinxinzi 欣欣子
Xiuta yeshi 绣榻野史
Xu Changling 徐昌龄

Xu Wei 徐渭
Xuanzong 玄宗
xue 穴
Xue Aocao 薛敖曹
Xue Huaiyi 薛怀义

Yan Qiongke 燕筇客
Yanzai 延载
yang 阳
yangwu 阳物
Yang Zaisi 杨再思
Yang Zhirou 杨执柔
yin 阴
yinfang 阴房
yinhu 阴户
You hu 有狐
You xianku 游仙窟
Yuxuanji 鱼玄机
Yuan Hongdao 袁宏道
Yuantong 元统

Zhang Changzong 张昌宗
Zhang Dai 张岱
Zhang Liang 张良
Zhang Yizhi 张易之
Zhang Zhuo 张鷟
Zhao 曌
Zhaoge 朝歌
Zhaoyi 昭仪
Zheng-Wei 郑卫
Zhiyanzhai 脂胭斋
Zhongzong 中宗
Zhouwang 纣王
zhubing 麈柄
Zijin 子衿

Selected Bibliography

Works in English

Balzac, Honore. *Pere Goriot*. New York: W. W. Norton & Co. (1997).

Balzac, Honore. *Eugenie Grandet*. New York: Creative Space (2010).

Barzun, Jacques. *From Dawn to Decadence: 500 Years of Western Cultural Life*. New York: Harper-Collins (2000).

Chunshue. *Beijing Doll*. New York: Riverhead Trade (2004).

Cooney, Eleanor & Daniel Altieri. *Deception: A Novel of Murder and Madness in Tang China*. New York: William Morrow & Co. (1993).

d'Estree, Sabine, trans. *Story of O*. New York: Ballantine Books (1973).

Dolezelova-Velingerova, Milena. "The Narrative Mode in Late Qing Fiction." in Milena Dolezelova-Velingerova, ed., *The Chinese Novel at the Turn of Century*. Toronto: University of Toronto Press (1981).

Feuerwerker, Yi-tsi Mei. *Ding Ling's Fiction: Ideology and Narrative in Modern Chinese Literature*. Cambridge: Harvard University Press (1982).

Glyn, Richard Jones & A. Susan Williams, eds. *Erotic Stories by Women*. London: Penguin Books (1996).

Guisso, R.W.L. *Wu Tse-t'ien and Politics of Legitimation in T'ang China*. Western Washington University Press (1978).

Hegel, Robert. *Reading Illustrated Fiction in Late Imperial China*. Stanford: Stanford University Press (1998).

Hsia, C.T. *The Classic Chinese Novel*. Bloomington: Indiana University Press (1968).

Hu, Lenny. *The Embroidered Couch*. Vancouver: Arsenal Pulp Press (2001).

Hu, Lenny & R.W.L. Guisso. *In the Inner Quarters: Erotic Stories from Ling Mengchu's Two Slaps*. Vancouver: Arsenal Pulp Press (2003).

Huang, Martin. *Desire and Fictional Narrative in Late Imperial China*. Cambridge: Harvard University Press (2001.

Ihara, Saikabu. *The Life of an Amorous Women and Other Writings*. Ed. & trans. By Ivan Morris. New York: New Direction 1963.

Ihara, Saikaku. *The Life of an Amorous Man*. Trans. Kengi Hamada. Boston: Tuttle Publishing Company (1963).

Ko, Dorothy. *Teachers of the Inner Chambers: Women and Culture in Seventeenth Century China*. Stanford: Stanford University Press (1995).

Kronhausen, Eberhard, and Phyllis Kronhausen. *Pornography and the Law: the Psychology of Erotic Realism and Pornography*. New York: Ballantine Books (1959).

Lau, D. C., trans. *The Analects*. London, Penguin Books (1979).

Mann, Susan. *Precious Records: Women in China's Long Eighteenth Century*. Stanford: Stanford University Press (1997).

Millet, Catherine. *The Sexual Life of Catherine* M., trans. Adriana Hunter. New York: Grove Press (2002).

Min, Anchee. *Wild Ginger*. New York: Mariner Books (2002).

Moi, Toril. "Feminist, Female, Feminine", in *The Feminist Reader*, eds., Catherine Belsey & Jane Moore. New York: Basil Blackwell (1989).

Moulton, Ian Frederick, trans. *The Book of the Prick*. New York: Routledge (2003).

Needham, Joseph. *Science and Civilization in China*, vol. 11. Cambridge: Cambridge University Press (1954).

Owen, Stephen, ed. *Anthology of Chinese Literature*. New York: W. W. Norton & Company (1996).

Plaks, Andrew. *The Four Masterworks of the Ming Novel*. Princeton: Princeton University Press (1987).

Rouzer, Paul. *The Articulated Ladies: Gender and the Male Community in the Early Chinese Texts.* Cambridge, Massachusetts: Harvard University Press (2001).

Roy, David, trans. *Plum in the Golden Vase*. Princeton: Princeton University Press (1992–2006).

Showalter, Elaine. "The Feminist Critical Revolution", in Elaine Showalter, ed., *The New Feminist Criticism: Essays on Women, Literature, and Theory*. New York: Pantheon Books (1985).

Siedensticker, Edward, trans. *The Tale of Genji*. New York: Vintage Classics Edition (1990).

Stone, Charles. *The Fountainhead of Chinese Erotica: Lord of Perfect Satisfaction*. Hawaii: University of Hawaii Press (2003).

Tang, Xianzu. *Peony Pavilion*, trans. Cyril Birch. Bloomington: Indiana University Press (2002).

Twitchett, Denis, et al, eds. *Cambridge History of China: Volume 3, Sui and Tang China.* Cambridge: Cambridge University Press (1979).

Twittchett, Denis & Frederick Mote, eds. *Cambridge History of China: Ming Dynasty*. Cambridge: Cambridge University Press (1988).

Van Gulik, Robert. *Sexual Life in Ancient China*. Leiden: Brill Academic Publishers (2003).

Warren, Marcus. "Sex with a Sexagenarian", in *The Vancouver Sun*, May 12, 2003.

Wile, Douglas. *Art of the Bedchamber*. Albany: State University of New York Press (1992).

Wills, Gary, trans. *Saint Augustine's Memory*. New York: Viking (2002).

Yang, Yeeshan. *Whispers and Moans: Interviews with Men and Women of Hong Kong's Sex Industry*. New York: Blacksmith Books (2010).

Works in Chinese

Cihai 辞海 (Sea of Words). Shanghai: Cishu chubanshe (1980).

Hu, Lingyi 胡令毅. "Chipozi zhuan de zuozhe wenti" 痴婆子传的作者问题 (On the Authorship of Crazy Old Woman), in *Ming-Qing xiaoshuo yanjiu* 明清小说研究 (Journal of Studies of Ming-Qing Fiction), 2006, no.1.

——. "Lun Xinmen Qing de yuanxing" 论西门庆的原型 (On the Real Identity of Ximen Qing), in *Henan daxue xuebao* 河南大学学报 (Journal of Henan University), 2006, no. 1.

——. "Lun Meng Yulou" 论孟玉楼 (On Meng Yulou), in *Xuzhou gongcheng xueyuan xuebao* 徐州工程学院学报 (Journal of Xuzhou College of Technology), 2007, no. 3.

——. "Lun Xu Wei he Jin Ping Mei" 论徐渭和金瓶梅 (On Xu Wei and the Plum in the Golden Vase), in *Henan daxue xuebao* (Journal of Henan University), 2007, no. 5.

——. "Jin Ping Mei li de yingsu zhi wen" 金瓶梅里的应俗之文 (Practical Writings in the Plum in the Golden Vase), in *Luoyang shifan xueyang xuebao* 洛阳师范学院学报 (Journal of Luoyang Teachers' College), 2007, no. 6.

——. "Lun Wen xiucai" 论温秀才 (On Licentiate Wen), in *Xuzhou gongcheng xueyuan xuebao* (Journal of Xuzhou College of Technology), 2008, no. 1.

Huang, Lin黄霖. "*Chipozi zhuan*" (Memoir of a Crazy Old Woman), in Zhang Peiheng et al., *Zhongguo jinshu daguan* 中国禁书大全 (Compendium of Banned Books in China). Shanghai: Wenhua chubanshe (1990).

Huang, Xun 黄训. *Dushu yide* 读书一得 (A Gleaning from Reading Books). Publisher unknown.

Ji, Wenfu嵇文甫. *Wan-Ming sixiang shilun*明代思想史论 (Historical Interpretation of Late Ming Thought). Beijing: Dongfang chubanshe (1996).

Ji, Yougong 计有功. *Tangshi jishi* 唐诗记事 (Events Behind the Compilation of Tang Poetry). Beijing: Zhonghua shuju (2007).

Lei, Jiaji雷家骥. *Humei pianneng huozhu*狐媚偏能惑主(Only her Foxy Fascination Could Captivate her Master. Taipei: Lianming wenhua youxian gongsi (1982).

——. *Wu Zetian zhuan* 武则天传 (Biography of Wu Zetian). Beijing: Renmin chuban she (2001).

Liu, Hui刘辉. "*Ruyijun zhuan* de kanke niandai jiqi yu *Jin Ping Mei* zhi guanxi" 如意君传得刊刻年代及 其与金瓶梅之关系(Lord of Perfect Satisfaction: The Year of its Publication and its Relationship with The Plum in the Golden Vase), in *Xuzhou Shifan xueyuan xuebao* 徐州师范学院学报(Journal of Xuzhou Normal University), No. 3, 1987.

Lu Xun 鲁迅, *Zhongguo xiaoshuo shilue* 中国小说史略 (A Brief History of Chinese Fiction), in *Lu Xun quanji* 鲁迅全集 (Complete Works of Lu Xun. Beijing: Renmin wenxue chubanshe (1989).

Li, Mengsheng李梦生. "*Chipozi zhuan*" (Memoir of a Crazy Old Woman), in Li Mengsheng, *Zhongguo jinhui xiaoshuo baihua*中国禁毁小说百话 (A Hundred Topics on the Banned Books in China. Shanghai: Guiji chubanshe (1994).

——. "*Ruyijun zhuan*" (Lord of Perfect Satisfaction), in Li Mengsheng, *Zhongguo jinhui xiaoshuo baihua* (A Hundred Topics on the Banned Books in China. Shanghai: Guiji chubanshe (1994).

Li, Shiren 李时人. "*Chipozi zhuan*: Sibainian qian de yibu rensheng canhui lu" 痴婆子传: 四百年前的一 部人生忏悔录 (Memoir of a Crazy Old Woman: A Four-Hundred-Year-Old Confession), in Li Shiren et al., *Zhongguo gudai jinhui xiaoshuo manhua* 中国古代禁毁小说漫话 (Informal Discourses on the Banned Books in Ancient China. Shanghai: Hanyudacidian chubanshe (1999).

——. "*Ruyijun zhuan*: Ming-Qing tongsu xiaoshuo xing miaoxie zhi lanshang" 如意君传: 明清通俗小 说性描写之滥觞 (Lord of Perfect Satisfaction: the Beginning of Sexual Description in Ming-Qing Fiction), in Li Shiren et al., *Zhongguo gudai jihui xiaoshuo manhua* (Informal Discourses on the Banned Books in Ancient China. Shanghai: Hanyu dacidian chubanshe (1999).

Ma, Meixin 马美信. "Wan Ming wenxue chutan" 晚明文学初探 (A Preliminary Study of Late Ming Literature), in *Zhongguo shoupi wenxue boshi xuewei lunwen xuanji* 中国首批文学博士学位论 文选集(The First Selection of PhD Dissertations on Literature. Jinan: Shandong daxue chubanshe (1987).

Ouyang, Xiu欧阳修, et al. *Xin Tang shu* 新唐书 (New History of the Tang. Beijing, Zhonghua shuju (1997).

Qi Gong, *Lunshu jueju* (Quatrains on Calligraphy. Beijing: Sanlian shudian (1990).

Shen, Defu 沈德符. *Wanli yehuo bian* 万历野获编 (Unofficial Records of the Wanli Reign). Beijing: Zhonghua shuju (1997).

Sima, Guang司马光. *Zizhi tongjian*资治通鉴 (Comprehensive Mirror for Aid in Government. Beijing, Zhonghua shuju (1987).

Sima, Qian 司马迁. ***Shiji*** 史记 (Records of the Grand Historian. Beijing, Zhonghua shuju, (1976).

Wang, Xiaotao王晓涛. Preface to "Lord of Perfect Satisfaction", in *Mingdai xiaoshuo jikan disan ji*明代 小说辑刊第三集(Fiction of the Ming Dynasty, Series 3. Chengdu, Bashu shushe (1997).

Wang, Xingqi王星圻. "*Chipozi zhuan* fafu" 痴婆子传发覆 (Reevaluation of the Memoirs of a Crazy Old Woman), in *Ming-Qing xiaoshuo yanjiu* (Journal of Studies of Ming-Qing Fiction) 1995, no. 1.

Wang Diwu 王棣武. *Wu Zetian shidai* 武则天时代 (The Era of Wu Zetian). Xiamen: Xiamen University (1991).

Wu, Cuncun 吴存存, "*Chipozi zhuan* yu nuxing zongyu de shizhi xing beiju" 痴婆子传与女性纵欲的实 质性悲剧 (Memoir of a Crazy Old Woman and the Real Tragedy of Female Sexual Indulgence), in *Ming-Qing shehui xing'ai fengqi* 明清社会性爱风气 (Sexual Practice in Ming-Qing Society). Beijing: Renmin wenxue chubanshe (2000).

Xia, Xianchun夏咸淳. *Wan-Ming shifeng yu wenxue* 晚明士风与文学 (The Mood of Literati and Literature in Late Ming). Beijing: Shehui kexue chubanshe (1994).

Xiao, Xiangkai肖相恺. "*Chipozi zhuan*" (Memoirs of a Crazy Old Woman), in Xiao Xiangkai, *Zhenben jinhui xiaoshuo daguan* 珍本禁毁小说大观 (Compendium of the Rare Versions of the Banned Books). Zhengzhou: Zhongzhou guji, (1992).

——. "*Ruyijun zhuan* liangzhong" 如意君传两种 (Two Versions of Lord of Perfect Satisfaction), in Xiao Xiangkai, *Zhenben jinhui xiaoshuo daguan* (Compendium of the Rare Editions of the Banned Books). Zhengzhou: Zhongzhou guji (1992).

Yue, Shi 乐史. *Guang zhuoyi ji* 广卓异记 (Expanded records of the Things Strange and Extraordinary). Yangzhou: Jiangsu guji chubanshe (1995).

Zhang, Peiheng章培恒. "Lord of Perfect Satisfaction", in Zhang Peiheng, et al. eds., *Zhongguo jinshu daguan* (Compendium of the Banned Books in China). Shanghai, Wenhua chubanshe (1990).

ASIAN THOUGHT AND CULTURE

This series is designed to cover three inter-related projects:

- *Asian Classics Translation*, including those modern Asian works that have been generally accepted as "classics"
- *Asian and Comparative Philosophy and Religion*, including excellent and publishable Ph.D. dissertations, scholarly monographs, or collected essays
- *Asian Thought and Culture in a Broader Perspective*, covering exciting and publishable works in Asian culture, history, political and social thought, education, literature, music, fine arts, performing arts, martial arts, medicine, etc.

For additional information about this series or for the submission of manuscripts, please contact:

Peter Lang Publishing, Inc.
Acquisitions Department
29 Broadway, 18th floor
New York, New York 10006

To order other books in this series, please contact our Customer Service Department at:

800-770-LANG (within the U.S.)
(212) 647-7706 (outside the U.S.)
(212) 647-7707 FAX

Or browse online by series at:

www.peterlang.com